美國家庭 天天說的
親子英語

Aman Chiu 著

新雅文化事業有限公司
www.sunya.com.hk

以**美國家庭**的方式學習！

Useful Expressions 活學活用

這裏額外舉出幾個美國家庭還會説的獨立情境，提供更多中英對照的實用對話，讓父母和孩子面對各種情況都能應付自如！

Theme 學習主題

本書包含 15 個學習主題，從孩子起牀到睡覺，上學到休假的生活細節，共 120 個場景，應有盡有！

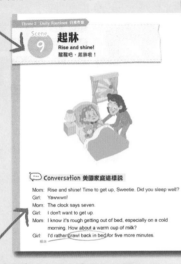

Conversation 美國家庭這樣説

這些都是美國家庭日常生活中常用的真實對話，配以生動有趣的插圖，可以邊看邊跟着對話來聊天！先培養英語語感，再掃描右邊的二維碼（QR Code），在網上查看中文翻譯的內容。

掃一掃！
網上中文版

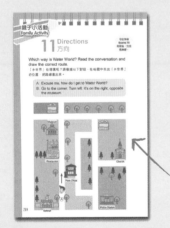

親子生活互動遊戲，學習英語樂在其中！

本書設 18 個 Family Activity 親子小活動，家長和孩子實踐英語對話後，可按不同的主題使用相關的活動。家長可先説出英語指令，然後與孩子一起動動手，完成各個有趣又好玩的活動，讓孩子鞏固所學！

★快樂學英語

透過遊戲創造説英語的語境，親子一同體驗學習英語的趣味！

英語這樣學，效果最顯著！

二維碼 QR Code

只要使用智能手機或平板電腦等設備，在連接網絡的狀態下掃描二維碼（QR Code），便可收聽美國人說出地道的英語，練習英語會話！

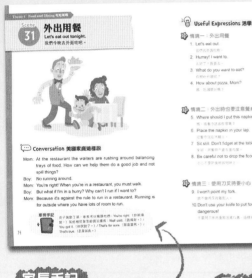

英文能力 UP！

解讀英語文法或特殊用法，提升孩子的英文能力！

家長手記

把英語學習結合品格教養，幫助父母用英語教育孩子。

西方文化 GoGoGo！

說好英語不等於融入了地道的外國生活！孩子具備西方文化的思維，說英語時更有自信！

詞彙手帳隨身帶，建立英語資料庫！

隨書附送 8 張雙面印刷的英語詞彙卡，包含 15 個學習主題，收錄約 230 個詞彙。家長和孩子可把它剪下來隨身攜帶，隨時隨地學好英語！

★圖像加深記憶

透過插圖學習英語詞彙，深深刻進孩子的記憶中，讓他們在任何情境也有充足的詞彙！

剪下來！

學習英語，可以很易，也可以很難。

許多學生從幼兒園到中學，學了超過十年的英語，還是覺得英語很難，在日常生活中也難以運用英語來表達思想感情，從而產生很大的挫敗感。久而久之，甚至對英語產生抗拒，最後放棄學習。對於他們來說，英語太難了。

在我住的大廈裏有一戶人家，一家四口，爸爸是法國人，媽媽是上海人，兩個小孩，姐姐快五歲了，弟弟還不到三歲。兩小姐弟除了一口流利的法語和普通話，還能操地道的英語和純正的廣東話，他們似乎擁有比一般孩子更強更驚人的語言能力。對於他們來說，學好一種語言毫不吃力，看來就是一件一蹴而就的事情。

為什麼有些孩子上了十幾年的英語課，還沒有足夠的信心說英語；有些幼兒仍未正式上學，卻能滔滔不絕地用不同語言跟別人交談？究竟，難易之間，問題出在哪裏？

很多研究結果都指向一個方向，要孩子學好外語，不能完全依靠學校和機構，家庭教育對孩子的學習效果起着至關重要的作用。學校的課堂既短暫又公式化，相對來說，家庭教育能夠打破空間和時間的界限，所能發揮的作用就更大了。身邊有家長朋友非常注重家庭語言學習，他們的孩子英語能力特別強，並能考進一流的學校。父母是孩子的第一位老師，也是最重要的老師，能在自己家裏和日常生活中為小孩創造一個學習英語的環境，那是學好英語的一個重要起點。

本書的設計目的，就是要協助家長在家創造良好的英語學習氣氛，讓語言教學回歸生活——在生活中學，為生活而用，讓孩子打好學習的基礎。

要給孩子在家創造英語環境，首先要注意三個原則。

第一，培養聽說技能。幼兒學習語言以「習得」為主，即在成人與幼兒自然而然的語言交流與互動中逐步掌握語言。孩子小時候，英文只學聽說，不學讀寫，目的是要培養英語語感，建構英語思維，打下學習語言的穩健基礎。聽說熟悉後，再學拼讀及其後的讀寫等就快很多了。

第二，緊貼實際生活。不脫離生活，不揠苗助長。以輕鬆、自然的方式引導孩子在實際生活中應用會話，激發孩子的英語興趣，絕不會逼着孩子學。從而培養孩子用英語交流，並導向用英語進行簡單的思維能力。

第三，浸泡式學習環境。幼齡期的孩子學習外語時具有母語本能反應的特徵，大腦對接收到的英語毋須翻譯作母語就能理解。家長可以每天與孩子互動半個小時，讓他們沉浸在一個純粹的英語環境中。只要不斷重複，大量曝光在英語環境下，兒童就能像學母語一樣，自然學懂另一種語言。

三至六歲是孩子學習第二語言的黃金時期，只要找對了方法，堅持培養，加上持之以恆的鍛煉，在家學習，也能取得成功。

Aman Chiu

目錄 Content

Theme 5 Household Chores
做做家務

Theme 6 Relaxing at Home
居家娛樂

親子小活動
Family Activity

詞彙手帳 Vocabulary

Theme 1 - 15

Scene 1 成長

You're a big boy now.
你已經長大了。

 Conversation 美國家庭這樣說

Boy:　Mom, this shirt is very cute.

Mom:　Ha ha, this is the shirt you wore when you were a baby.

Boy:　Oh, it was my shirt?

Mom:　Yes!

Boy:　Why can't I recall any of this?

Mom:　You were just a baby. You were much too young to remember. You're a big boy now.

 家長手記　You're a big boy / girl now. 是美國家長不時用上的一句話，能讓兒童在成長過程中獲得自信、勇氣和上進心。例如當孩子長大了還在吮手指，你就可以跟他說：Come on, you're a big boy now. 孩子還那麼膽小？你可以說：You're a big boy now, you should be brave.（要勇敢啊！）要孩子幫忙做些事情，可以說：You're a big boy now. Can you help Mom?（可以幫幫媽媽嗎？）

Useful Expressions 活學活用

聆聽英文內容

 情境一：孩子長高了

1. Let's see how tall you are.
   來看看你有多高。

2. Wow! You've grown quite a bit!
   哇！你已經長大了好多喔！

3. I want to be taller.
   我想再高一點。

4. I wish I could be taller.
   我希望我再高一點就好了。

 英文能力 UP！

I wish I could 屬於虛擬語氣，說話者但願某事已發生，可是卻事與願違。

 情境二：成長的疑惑

5. Mom, am I growing normally?
   媽，我生長得正常嗎？

6. Why am I not as tall as my friend?
   為什麼我沒有我的朋友那樣高？

7. Kids come in a wide range of shapes and sizes.
   And they don't grow at a steady rate, either.
   小孩子的高矮肥瘦都不一樣，成長的速度也不是一模一樣呀。

8. Some people grow late. Some people grow early.
   有些人長得比較慢，有些人長得快一些。

情境三：給予正面的回應

9. Your height is just average for your age.
   以你的年齡來說，你的身高是正常的。

10. You'll grow more if you eat well.
    如果你好好吃飯的話，你會長得更快。

11. You need to drink milk to grow taller.
    你要多喝牛奶，才能長得更高。

Scene 2

體重

Step on the scale.
站在磅秤上。

💬 Conversation 美國家庭這樣說

Mom:　Come on, Sweetie. Step on the scale.

Girl:　Oh my goodness! I've gained 5 kilograms in a month. I think
　　　I feel like a huge marshmallow!

Mom:　Yes, you've put on a few kilograms. It happens, and it's fine.

Girl:　Mom, I just can't seem to get back to how I was. You know?
　　　My friends call me a fatty. 胖子，含貶義

西方文化 GoGoGo!

美國人常常用 Oh my goodness!（天哪！/ 哎呀！）來表示
驚訝。它還有一些變體，例如 Oh my gosh! / Gosh! / Gee! /
Jeez! 等，意思都是一樣的。這其實都是 Oh my God! 或 Oh
my Jesus! 的委婉說法，人們避免直呼上帝的名字，以免冒犯
有宗教信仰的人。

Useful Expressions 活學活用

 情境一：量體重

1. Let's measure your weight.

   我們來量一下你的體重。

2. I weigh 23 kg.

   我的體重是 23 公斤。

3. You've gained / lost weight.

   你的體重增加了 / 減少了。

4. You weigh a lot / a little.

   你很重 / 不怎麼重。

 情境二：長胖了

5. You're a little chubby / plump.

   你有點胖。

6. Am I overweight, Mom?

   媽，我過重了嗎？

7. You're adorable the way you are.

   你這樣就很可愛了。

8. I need some exercise to lose weight.

   我需要運動來減肥。

9. I will try to eat less from now on.

   現在開始，我試着少吃一點。

西方文化 GoGoGo!

在美國，用 fat 來指人肥胖的話，會讓人家生氣。禮貌些可以說 plump 或 chubby，兩者都是用來指人「豐滿」，有「胖得可愛」的意思。

 情境三：長得太瘦了

10. Am I too thin?

    我很瘦嗎？

11. You're slim.

    你很苗條。

17

自己睡的晚上

Go to sleep in your room.

去自己的房間睡吧。

💬 Conversation 美國家庭這樣說

Mom: Time for bed! Brush your teeth, and then get in bed.

Girl: Mom, I'm feeling scared to sleep in my room.

Mom: That's okay. **Now that** you're grown up, go to sleep in
　　　　　　　　　　　　　　　　　　　　　　　　　　長大了
your room. I will leave the door open and turn on your
night light. And I will pop in later to check on you. Okay?
Good night, Sweetie.　過來一下

Girl: Good night, Mom.

英文能力 UP！

Now that 是連接詞，指既然、由於，用來表示原因或理由，例如：Now
that I live near my school, I walk to school every day.（由於我住得很近學
校，我可以每天走路上學。）

Useful Expressions 活學活用

聆聽英文內容

 情境一：不願一個人睡

1. Mom, I'm scared. I can't go to sleep by myself.

   媽，我好害怕，我沒辦法自己一個人睡。

2. Mom, don't turn off the light.

   媽，不要關燈。

3. I want to sleep with you.

   我要跟你一起睡。

4. Now that you're a big boy / girl, go to sleep in your room.

   你已經長大了，去自己的睡房睡。

 情境二：陪着孩子入睡

5. Will you stay with me until I go to sleep?

   你可以待到我去睡覺嗎？

6. Want me to sing you to sleep?

   要我唱歌哄你睡嗎？

7. Don't worry. Mom will be with you.

   不用擔心，媽媽會跟你在一起。

情境三：哄孩子睡覺

8. Let's cuddle a minute together before we turn out the lights.

   我們抱着睡一分鐘，然後就關燈。

9. If you stay in bed without calling out to us, you'll have your favorite surprise at breakfast in the morning.

   如果你睡覺時沒有喊我們，那麼明天早上吃早餐時就會有驚喜的呀。

家長手記

分開睡不能完全參照兒童的年齡來劃一個分界線，而是根據孩子的實際情況、家庭居住情況而定。如果孩子自理能力較強，例如晚上睡得安穩、不亂踢被子等，家長此時就可以給孩子準備房間了。

Scene 4

第一天上學

Are you ready for school?
你準備好去上學了嗎？

💬 Conversation 美國家庭這樣說

Mom:　You'll go to school from now on. Are you excited about going to school?

Girl:　I'm excited, but I'm <mark>kinda</mark> scared, too.

Mom:　You're a big girl now and not a baby anymore. Look at my sweetie in her uniform. Do you like your new school clothes?

Girl:　They're nice.

Mom:　Good. You look adorable. Mommy will take you to school today. Are you ready for school?

Girl:　Yes, I'm ready.

> **英文能力 UP！**
>
> Kinda 是 kind of 的口語形式，表示有點兒的意思，例如：I'm kinda scared.（我有點兒害怕。）又如：He is kinda shy, isn't he?（他有點兒害羞，不是嗎？）

20

Useful Expressions 活學活用

聆聽英文內容

 ### 情境一：準備上學了

1. You're starting kindergarten soon. Are you ready?

   你要上幼兒園了，你準備好了嗎？

2. Mom, I'm ready for school!

   媽，我準備好去上學了！

3. Have you got everything?

   東西都帶了嗎？

4. I got everything ready.

   我都準備好了。

美國的免費教育稱為 K-12，也就是從 kindergarten（幼兒園）一直到 12th Grade（高中）。每個州的入學規定都不同，大部分規定入學年齡為 5 歲，至少要讀到 18 歲高中畢業。

 ### 情境二：孩子鬧彆扭時

5. Mom, I don't want to go.

   媽，我不想去。

6. I'm nervous.

   我很緊張。

 ### 情境三：安撫鬧情緒的孩子

7. Don't be nervous. Your teacher is going to take care of you.

   不要緊張，你的老師會照顧你。

8. It's okay to be afraid. But, you'll feel better each day that you're there. Lots of kids feel just like you do.

   害怕也不要緊，你在那裏會一天一天的好起來，很多小朋友都跟你一樣有這種感覺。

9. You're not alone.

   你不是一個人的。

10. You're going to make new friends.

    你會交到新朋友的。

Scene 5

換牙了
Are my teeth falling out, Mom?
媽，我要掉牙了嗎？

💬 Conversation 美國家庭這樣說

Boy:　Woowoyoyaahh…

Mom:　What are you talking about?

Boy:　My tooth is shaking and wobbly.

Mom:　What happened? Let me have a look. Open your mouth.

Boy:　Are my teeth falling out, Mom?

Mom:　Oh, I see. That's why you can't speak clearly. It's time to replace your current milk teeth with permanent teeth. It means that you're growing up.

英文能力 UP！

Oh 是感歎詞，表示說話者對某事感到意外或驚訝，常常與一些單詞或詞組連用，有時表明說話者「明白了、知道了」，例如 Oh, I see. / Oh, yes. / Oh, all right. / Oh, okay.

Useful Expressions 活學活用

聆聽英文內容

 ## 情境一：換牙帶來的麻煩

1. I've got a loose tooth.

   我有一顆牙齒快掉了。

2. It's hard to chew because some of my teeth are missing.

   因為有些牙齒掉了，咀嚼起來很困難。

 ## 情境二：換牙是正常的事情

3. I'm never going to let my tooth fall out.

   我絕對不會讓我的牙齒掉下來。

4. It's normal for you to lose a tooth. You are entering the tooth transition period.

   你已經進入換牙期，掉牙齒是正常不過的事情。

 ## 情境三：換牙的疑惑

5. Why do we need tooth transition?

   我們為什麼需要換牙？

6. From the time when you were a baby to the age of two, twenty teeth grew in your mouth. They are called milk teeth.

   從我們嬰兒時期至大約兩歲時，口腔會長出二十顆牙齒，這些牙齒稱為乳齒。

7. When you grow older, the tiny milk teeth are not good enough for you anymore.

   我們日漸長大，細小的乳齒已不再適合了。

8. So they begin to fall out one after another. Then, permanent teeth will gradually grow in.

   於是乳齒開始逐一脫落，然後恆齒就會漸漸長出來。

Scene 6

自己來刷牙

It's time to brush your teeth!

是時候刷牙了！

 Conversation 美國家庭這樣說

Mom: Honey, it's time to brush your teeth! Let's get them nice and clean.

Boy: I hate brushing my teeth. Can you brush them for me?

Mom: I know it's hard to brush your teeth, but if you don't take care of your teeth, you'll get cavities.

Boy: Oh, I don't want to get cavities!

Mom: Then brush your teeth, and then get in bed.

Tooth Fairy（牙仙子）是美國一則美麗的童話，傳說如果孩子有牙齒脫落，牙仙子就會悄悄把牙齒拿走，並用這些美麗的牙齒為精靈搭建宮殿。但是牙仙子只取沒有蛀過的牙齒，所以小朋友要好好保護自己的牙齒啊！

Useful Expressions 活學活用

聆聽英文內容

 情境一：孩子不願刷牙時

1. I hate brushing my teeth.

   我討厭刷牙。

2. Brush my teeth for me, Mom.

   媽，幫我刷牙。

3. If you don't brush well, your teeth will turn black!

   如果你不好好刷牙的話，你的牙齒就會變成黑色！

 情境二：刷牙的步驟

4. Squeeze the toothpaste for me, Mom.

   媽，幫我擠牙膏。

5. Put only a little toothpaste on your toothbrush.

   擠一點點牙膏在牙刷上就可以。

6. Gently brush up and down.

   要輕輕地上下刷。

7. Don't forget to brush inside.

   不要忘記刷牙齒的內側。

8. Clean your teeth and gums thoroughly.

   牙齒和牙牀都要徹底地刷乾淨。

9. Brush for three minutes.

   刷三分鐘。

10. Don't leave the water running.

    不要忘記關水。

11. Do I also need to brush my tongue?

    舌頭也要刷嗎？

12. Gargle and spit.

    用水漱口，然後把水吐掉。

Scene 7

自己穿衣服

Can you get dressed by yourself?

你能自己穿衣服嗎？

💬 Conversation 美國家庭這樣說

Mom: Can you get dressed alone today? You'd be such a big boy.

Boy: OK, I'll put my shirt on.

Mom: Good. Put your arms out. That's right, one arm at a time.

Boy: I can do the buttons up. 把鈕扣扣好

Mom: Great! Well done for putting your shirt on, that's a big help!

家長手記　Well done!（做得不錯！做得好！做得真好！）是用來讚美對方做得很好的固定口語表達形式。每個人都希望被別人肯定，孩子也不例外。如果家長表揚、讚美或認同孩子積極的一面，就能鼓勵他們繼續往好的方面發展。家長讚美孩子做得好的說法還有 Good job! 和 Way to go!

Useful Expressions 活學活用

聆聽英文內容

 ## 情境一：自己穿衣服

1. You're a big boy now, you can dress yourself.
   你已經長大了，該能自己穿衣服了。
2. Let's get changed.
   我們來換衣服吧。
3. I can put on the clothes by myself.
   我可以自己穿上衣服。

 ## 情境二：家長從旁引導

4. Let's button your shirt.
   把襯衫的鈕扣扣好。
5. Do the zips up. / Let's zip up your pants.
   把拉鏈拉好。／來把你褲子的拉鏈拉好。
6. Fold your sleeves.
   把袖子摺起來。
7. Let's put on your socks / shoes.
   來把襪子／鞋子穿上。

 家長手記

讓孩子自行穿衣，能培養他們的自理能力和增強自信心。但孩子起初手腳可能比較笨拙，家長不妨耐心一點教導。

 ## 情境三：請別人幫幫忙

8. Can you unbutton my shirt?
   你可以幫我解開襯衫的鈕扣嗎？
9. Can you unzip me?
   你可以幫我拉開拉鏈嗎？

 ## 情境四：把穿衣變成樂趣

10. I'll close my eyes and see how long it takes you to put on your shirt and pants.
    我先閉上眼睛，看看你用多少時間把襯衫和褲子穿好。

27

Scene 8 自己上廁所

Did you also wipe your bottom?
擦好你的屁股了嗎？

💬 Conversation 美國家庭這樣說

Mom: Stop what you're doing. Come back to the bathroom.

Boy: What happened, Mom?

Mom: Look behind when you're done!

Boy: Oh sorry!

擦屁股

Mom: How many times do I have to tell you to flush the toilet after use, huh?! Did you also wipe your bottom and wash your hands?

Boy: Oh…!!!

西方文化 GoGoGo!

美國家庭十分注重培養幼童的自理能力和良好衛生習慣。孩子入讀幼兒園時，校長或老師都會問家長有沒有對小孩進行 potty training（如廁訓練）。如不會自己上廁所、擦屁股，小朋友是不能入園的。

28

Useful Expressions 活學活用

聆聽英文內容

 情境一：上廁所

1. I have to pee / poop.

   我要去尿尿／便便。

2. Pull down your pants.

   把褲子脫下來。

3. Get onto the toilet.

   坐上馬桶。

4. Is it not coming out?

   排不出來嗎？

5. I'm done, Mom.

   媽，我上完廁所了。

6. Phew! It stinks!

   唷！好臭啊！

> **英文能力 UP！**
>
> Phew 是歎詞，表示討厭或聞到臭氣時的反應。

 情境二：做個清潔好孩子

7. Get some toilet paper, but don't take too much.

   拿些衛生紙，但不要用太多。

8. Can you wipe my bottom, Mommy?

   媽媽，您可以幫我擦屁股嗎？

9. Do a good job wiping.

   擦好屁股。

10. Don't forget to flush.

    不要忘記沖廁。

11. I'll flush the toilet after I pee / poop.

    我在尿尿／便便後會沖廁。

12. Wash your hands thoroughly.

    把手洗乾淨。

Scene
9

起牀

Rise and shine!

醒醒吧，起牀啦！

💬 Conversation 美國家庭這樣説

Mom: Rise and shine! Time to get up, Sweetie. Did you sleep well?

Girl: Yawwwn!

Mom: The clock says seven.

Girl: I don't want to get up.

Mom: I know it's rough getting out of bed, especially on a cold morning. How about a warm cup of milk?

Girl: I'd rather crawl back in bed for five more minutes.

賴牀

家長手記

在美國，很多家長會用 Rise and shine! 這句話來催促孩子趕快起牀。Rise and shine! 的表面意思是指太陽升起、陽光在照射，中文可以説成：「太陽曬到屁股啦！」或「醒醒吧，起牀啦！」

Useful Expressions 活學活用

 聆聽英文內容

 情境一：催促孩子起牀

1. It's almost time to get up.
   是時候起牀了。

2. Are you awake?
   你醒了嗎？

3. Wake up, sleepy head.
   起牀了，貪睡鬼。

4. Are you up yet?
   你起牀了嗎？

 情境二：還是不想起牀

5. I'm still sleepy. Can I sleep more?
   我還是很睏，我可以多睡一會兒嗎？

6. I'm so tired that I can't get up.
   我太累了，起不了牀。

 情境三：已經醒過來了

7. I'm already up.
   我已經醒了。

8. You don't need to wake me up.
   你不用叫我了。

 情境四：勸告懶惰的孩子

9. You should go to bed early to get up early.
   你要早睡早起。

 西方文化 GoGoGo!

我們在早上，一般只説句「早晨」。但美國人起牀後，通常會問候家人睡得好不好（Sleep well?），然後互相祝福對方有美好的一天（Have a nice day!）。

31

Scene 10

洗臉

Go wash your face.
去洗臉。

 Conversation 美國家庭這樣說

Mom: Go and wash your face, honey.

Boy: Why do we need to wash our face?

Mom: Washing your face will clear away the dirt and oils on your face.

Boy: Can you help me, Mom?

Mom: Can you do it yourself? You're such a big boy now.

Boy: If I do it myself, I will get my clothes wet.

Mom: Just be careful. Are you done?　洗好了嗎

Boy: There's no towel, Mommy. Can you get me a towel?

家長手記
美國家長往往把自己心愛的孩子喚作 Honey（寶貝／親愛的）。其他相同的暱稱包括：Sweetie（親愛的／小甜心）、Sweetheart（小甜心）、Darling（心愛的）、Babe（寶貝）。

Useful Expressions 活學活用

聆聽英文內容

 情境一：養成洗臉好習慣

1. Get up to wash your face.
   起牀洗臉了。

2. Washing your face can help to keep your skin healthy.
   洗臉可以讓你的皮膚保持健康。

3. I wash my face in the morning and at night.
   我在早上和晚上都會洗臉。

 情境二：洗臉的步驟

4. First, splash some water on your face.
   首先，把水潑在臉上。

5. Then, lather up and cleanse your face.
   然後，用潔臉泡沫洗臉。

6. Rinse off the lather.
   把潔臉泡沫沖洗掉。

7. Wash your neck, too.
   脖子也要洗啊。

8. Pat your face and neck dry with a towel.
   用毛巾輕輕拍乾臉和脖子。

9. Can you help me, Mom?
   媽，您可以幫我嗎？

 情境三：洗完臉了

10. I'm done.
    我洗好了。

11. Do I look pretty after washing up?
    我洗完臉看上去漂亮嗎？

家長手記

孩子洗完臉以後，父母不妨多讚美孩子，並且鼓勵他們對自己說讚美的話，例如：I am clean.（我很乾淨），從而增加孩子的自信心。

Scene 11

梳頭髮

Let's comb your hair.

我們來梳頭髮吧。

💬 Conversation 美國家庭這樣說

Mom:　Let's comb your hair.

Girl:　I want my hair tied in a braid today. Can you help me, Mom?

Mom:　OK. Let me put your hair up first. Your hair has grown a lot. You need a haircut.

Girl:　Oh Mom, don't tie it too hard. That hurts!

英文能力 UP！

麻花辮在英美兩地的叫法各有不同：美國人叫 braid，英國人叫 plait。至於辮子的類型，除了一般的辮子（pigtails）以外，還有馬尾辮（ponytail）、雙馬尾（bunches）等。

Useful Expressions 活學活用

聆聽英文內容

 情境一：梳頭髮

1. Let me part your hair.
   讓我來幫你的頭髮分邊。

2. Your hair is fluffy.
   你的頭髮很蓬鬆。

3. Your hair is tangled up.
   你的頭髮都打結了。

4. Brush my hair gently, Mom.
   媽，輕輕地幫我梳頭髮。

 情境二：不同的髮型

5. Mom, can you tie my hair?
   媽，可以幫我綁頭髮嗎？

6. Tie my hair in pigtails.
   把我的頭髮綁成辮子吧。

7. I'll tie your hair prettily.
   我會把你的頭髮綁得很漂亮。

8. I don't like this style.
   我不喜歡這個髮型。

9. Do you want the bangs to grow?
   你要把瀏海留長嗎？

 情境三：要剪髮了

10. My hair is poking me in my eyes.
    Can you cut my bangs?
    我的頭髮戳到眼睛了，能幫我把瀏海剪一下嗎？

11. Let's go to the hair salon this Saturday.
    這個星期六，我們去理髮店吧。

英文能力 UP！

理髮店在英美兩地的叫法也不盡相同：美國人會說 hair salon，簡稱 salon；英國人則叫 the hairdresser's。而特別為男士而設的理髮店叫 barbershop，英式說法叫 the barber's。

Scene 12

挑衣服

What do you want to wear today?

你今天想穿什麼呢？

💬 Conversation 美國家庭這樣說

Mom: What do you want to wear today – the Doraemon costume or the Barbie?

Girl: I don't want to wear either one.

Mom: Then, do you want to wear the shirt with the butterfly or the shirt with the big hearts today?

Girl: I want the butterfly one.

Mom: OK. And would you like to wear your yellow boots or your blue sneakers today?

家長手記

有育兒專家指出，兒童自 3、4 歲開始會「自作主張」。家長可讓他們自行選擇喜愛的服飾，啟發孩子思考，培養他們的獨立能力（independence）與責任心（sense of responsibility）。

Useful Expressions 活學活用

聆聽英文內容

 情境一：給孩子選擇的自主權

1. What do you want to wear?

   你想要穿什麼呢？

2. I want to wear a skirt today.

   我今天要穿裙子。

3. What to wear today – the dinosaur T-shirt or the truck T-shirt?

   今天穿什麼好呢？恐龍 T 恤衫還是火車頭 T 恤衫呢？

4. I don't want to wear those T-shirts.

   我不想穿那些 T 恤衫。

 情境二：從旁觀察與指導

5. Would you rather wear your red sweater or your green one?

   你比較喜歡穿那件紅色的毛衣，還是綠色的？

6. I notice you picked your yellow shirt again. You like that shirt.

   我看到你又選了黃色的襯衫來穿，看來你很喜歡這件襯衫呀。

7. Which of these two skirts would you like to wear with this top?

   這兩條短裙中，你要穿哪一條來配這上衣呢？

8. Does the skirt match the shirt?

   這條短裙跟這件襯衫搭配嗎？

 情境三：多作讚美

9. Do I look good, Mom?

   媽，我看起來好看嗎？

10. This shirt looks perfect on you.

    這襯衫穿在你身上太好看了。

11. You look really nice!

    你看起來真好看！

Scene 13 睡午覺

You need to take a nap.
你需要小睡一下。

💬 Conversation 美國家庭這樣說

Boy: Mom, look! Anna is yawning again.

Mom: She needs a nap.

Boy: Why does she sleep all the time?

Mom: Because she's still a little baby. A little baby needs to sleep 16 to 20 hours a day.

Boy: I don't need to sleep that much.

Mom: But still you need to take a nap. You need to recharge or you will become very tired.

恢復體力

英文能力 UP！

連接詞 or 用來連接兩個句子，具有警告的意味。說話者給對方提出忠告，以避免發生某種壞的結果。例如：Hurry up or we'll be late.（抓緊時間，不然我們要遲到了。）

Useful Expressions 活學活用

聆聽英文內容

 ## 情境一：孩子要求小睡

1. Mom, I'm tired.
   媽，我累了。

2. I want to take a nap.
   我想小睡一下。

3. Do you want to rest?
   你要休息一下嗎？

4. You'll be all right after taking a nap.
   小睡以後，你就會沒事了。

家長手記

有針對 3 至 6 歲兒童羣體睡眠的研究發現，有的孩子在午睡後有更好的記憶力（memory recall）。兒童一旦缺乏睡眠，將無法集中注意力，或情緒變得反覆無常，容易發怒，而且不易安慰。

 ## 情境二：小睡前的準備

5. Let's take a nap for an hour.
   我們來小睡一個小時吧。

6. Go to the bathroom before you take a nap.
   小睡前要上一下廁所。

7. I don't have to pee, Mom. I already went.
   媽，我不用去尿尿，我去過了。

 ## 情境三：解釋小睡的好處

8. Mom, I can't sleep.
   媽，我睡不着。

9. You need to sleep more because you need a lot of energy.
   你要多睡一點，這是因為你需要很多能量。

10. Taking a nap is like recharging your brain.
    小睡一會就像替你的大腦充電。

Scene 14 洗澡

It's time to take a bath.

是時候洗澡了。

💬 Conversation 美國家庭這樣說

Mom: It's time to take a bath.

Boy: Mom, I want to wash my hair first.

Mom: OK. I'll wash your hair now. Get ready for the water…
and here it comes…Wheee!

Boy: Mom, the water's cold!

Mom: Is the water warm now?

Boy: Yes, the water's warm now.

英文能力 UP！

「洗澡」一般可說成 take a bath（美式英語）或 have a bath（英式英語）。Bath 在英式英語中可作動詞來用，例如：Have you bathed the baby yet?（你給嬰兒洗澡了嗎？）美式英語則是 bathe，例如：I bathe every day.（我每天洗澡。）

Useful Expressions 活學活用

聆聽英文內容

 情境一：準備洗澡

1. It's time to take a shower.
   是時候淋浴了。

2. Mom, I want to take a bath / shower by myself.
   媽，我想自己洗澡 / 淋浴。

3. The tub is filled.
   浴缸的水滿了。

> **英文能力 UP！**
>
> 「浴缸」的美式英語是 tub 或 bathtub，英式英語則是 bath。

 情境二：孩子不願洗澡時

4. I don't want to take a bath / shower.
   我不想洗澡 / 淋浴。

5. There are only a few more minutes of play time and then it's time for the tub, okay?
   只可以再玩幾分鐘，然後馬上要去洗澡，好嗎？

 情境三：洗澡時

6. Let me rub the soap and make some foam.
   我來搓肥皂弄些泡泡。

7. Let me wash off the soap.
   我來把肥皂洗掉。

8. Oh, no splashing the water!
   噢，不要潑水！

 情境四：洗完澡了

9. All done washing, now it's time to turn off the water.
   洗好了，現在把水關上。

10. Dry yourself with the towel.
    用毛巾把身體擦乾。

41

Scene 15

睡前故事

Let me read you a story.

我來給你說故事。

💬 Conversation 美國家庭這樣説

Mom: Let me read you a story. Mommy will read to you until you fall asleep. Choose a book you want to read.

Girl: This one.

Mom: You picked a good one. Listen carefully. You can listen with your eyes closed. Once upon a time, there was a very poor boy named Aladdin…

Girl: Yawwwn… I'm sleepy, Mom.

Mom: Okay, you can sleep if you feel sleepy.

西方文化 GoGoGo!

睡前閱讀是美國家庭的古老傳統，美國父母在白天有多忙多累也好，到了晚上只要有空閒時間，都會擁着被窩裏的孩子，給他們講述一個美妙動聽的故事。前美國教育部長瑞萊（Richard Riley）指出：「如果父母每天能夠花 30 分鐘來幫助孩子閱讀，對孩子的教育將有非常大的幫助。」

Useful Expressions 活學活用

聆聽英文內容

 情境一：睡前説故事

1. Mom, what are you going to read to me today?

   媽，您今天要説哪個故事呢？

2. Do you want me to read a story to you?

   要我給你説故事嗎？

3. Where did we read to yesterday?

   我們昨天説到哪裏呢？

 情境二：給孩子選擇的空間

4. Which book should we read before bed – this one or that one?

   我們睡覺前讀哪本書好呢？這本還是那本？

5. You chose too many. Pick one only.

   你選太多了，選一本就好。

6. This one.

   這一本。

7. Will you read this story to me again tomorrow?

   明天可以再説這個故事給我聽嗎？

 情境三：孩子不願睡覺或不願聽故事

8. Read me one more, Mom.

   媽，再講一個。

9. I'm not going to bed!

   我不要睡覺！

10. Okay, I guess you've chosen not to have a book tonight. Good night, Sweetie! We'll try again tomorrow night!

    好吧，看來你選擇今晚不聽故事了吧。晚安了，小甜心，我們明天晚上再説故事吧。

Scene 16

睡覺

It's bedtime already.
是睡覺的時間了。

💬 Conversation 美國家庭這樣説

Mom: It's getting too late and it's time for you to get ready for bed.

Boy: I don't want to go to bed.

Mom: I know you wish you could keep playing with your toys, but I'm afraid it's bedtime already.

Boy: I'm not tired yet.

Mom: It's almost ten. Go to bed! It'll be hard to get out of bed in the morning if you don't sleep enough. Good night! Mommy will kiss you.

西方文化 GoGoGo!

在非正式日常英語中，美國人在晚上睡覺前通常只説 Night! 對孩子説晚安的時候，家長多會説 Night night，例如：Night night, darling. See you in the morning.（晚安，寶貝，明天早上見。）

Useful Expressions 活學活用

聆聽英文內容

 情境一：要睡覺了

1. Time for bed!

   是時候睡覺了！

2. We need to go to bed. I am right here with you.

   我們要睡覺了，我會在這裏陪着你。

3. Let me tuck you in.

   我來幫你蓋被子。

4. Can you sing me a lullaby?

   可以給我唱搖籃曲嗎？

 情境二：催促孩子睡覺

5. Brush your teeth, and then get in bed.

   快去刷牙，然後上牀睡覺。

6. Mom, I'm not tired yet.

   媽，我還不睏。

7. I can't sleep. I want to go to sleep later.

   我睡不着，我要晚點睡。

8. When it's dark, we sleep. When it's light, Mommy and Daddy come to get you.

   天黑了就要睡，天亮的時候爸爸媽媽就會過來看你。

 情境三：互道晚安

9. Good night, Mom.

   媽，晚安。

10. Sweet dreams! Give Mommy a goodnight kiss. See you tomorrow!

    祝你有個好夢！睡前跟媽媽親親吧，明天見！

Scene 17

上學去

You'll be late for school.
上學要遲到了。

💬 Conversation 美國家庭這樣說

Mom: Hurry up, Sweetie! Mom's waiting. We've got to leave right now or you'll be late for school!

Girl: I'm coming, Mom.

Mom: Quick! Put on your shoes. Put on your jacket. Mommy will take you to school today.

Girl: All right. Let's go.

Mom: Shouldn't you say goodbye to Daddy?

英文能力 UP！

Shouldn't you 用於提醒，還帶有一點命令的口吻，例如：Shouldn't you say goodbye to Daddy?（你不是要跟爸爸說再見嗎？）或 You shouldn't have done that!（你不應該這樣做！）

Useful Expressions 活學活用

聆聽英文內容

 ## 情境一：準備上學

1. You're going to be late for school. You need to get dressed right now.

   你上學要遲到了，你馬上要穿好衣服。

2. Put on your school uniform. You have to be ready for school in 10 minutes!

   穿上校服，你要在 10 分鐘內準備好去上學！

 ## 情境二：還有時間，別緊張

3. We still have time, Mom.

   媽，我們還有時間。

4. If you're still lollygagging, we're all going to be late.

   你還是拖拖拉拉的話，我們大家都會遲到的。

5. I'm doing my best.

   我正在盡全力。

 ## 情境三：校門前道別

6. Bye, Mom!

   媽，再見！

7. Have fun, Sweetie!

   玩開心點，小甜心！

8. Have a good day!

   祝你有美好的一天！

9. Have fun with your friends.

   跟朋友好好玩呀。

10. Be happy all day long.

    一整天都要快樂呀。

家長手記

美國家庭會給上學定下 Have Fun（開心）的基調，讓孩子覺得上學是很有趣的事情。家長把子女送到學校時大多會說聲：Have fun, Sweetie! 接子女放學時又會說一句：Did you have fun at school today, honey? （今天在學校過得開心嗎，寶貝？）

47

Scene 18

坐校巴

The school bus is coming.
校巴來了。

💬 Conversation 美國家庭這樣說

Boy: Mom, what if I don't get off at school and end up somewhere else?

Mom: You can't miss the school.

Boy: Why?　　　　錯過　　　　　　最重要的工作

Mom: The school bus driver's number one job is to get every kid to school safely, so he'll check to make sure you do too.

Boy: The school bus is coming.

Mom: Okay, let's get on the school bus now.

英文能力 UP！

What if...? 的意思是「如果……將怎麼辦？」這個句型的完整結構是
What would happen if...? 或 What are you going to do if...? 它的省略
形式 What if...? 在口語中十分常見。

Useful Expressions 活學活用

聆聽英文內容

 情境一：校巴來了

1. The school bus will be here very soon.
   校巴馬上要來了。

2. I see the bus coming.
   我看到校巴來了。

3. Wait until the bus has stopped.
   要等校巴停好呀。

西方文化 GoGoGo!

在美國幼兒園裏，秩序是孩子第一件要學的事，排隊更是美國孩子的必修課。因此，老師常常會說：Line up, everybody!（大家排好隊！）離開教室，無論去哪裏他們都會排成一隊。

 情境二：遵守秩序

4. Let's line up nicely.
   我們好好排隊吧。

5. Don't cut in line.
   不要插隊。

6. Remain seated for the whole ride.
   全程都要坐好。

 情境三：上車時

7. Say "Good morning" to the driver.
   跟司機說早安。

8. I can fasten the seatbelt by myself.
   我能自己繫好安全帶。

英文能力 UP！

Fasten the seatbelt 的另一個說法是 Buckle the seatbelt up，簡稱為 Buckle up，在日常口語中較常用。

 情境四：下車時

9. Let's get off.
   我們下車了。

10. Wave goodbye to the driver.
    跟司機揮手說再見。

Scene 19

做功課

Have you done your homework?
你做完功課了嗎？

💬 Conversation 美國家庭這樣説

Mom: Sweetie, have you done your homework?

Boy: Not yet.

Mom: Start doing it now! Stop watching TV!

Boy: I don't have to do it because my teacher said we'll do it in class tomorrow.

Mom: Are you sure?

Boy: Hmmm…

Mom: No excuses. Do it anyway!

家長手記　當孩子隱瞞真相或故意推搪，逃避責任時，家長可以説：
No excuses!（不要找藉口！）相同的説法還有：No more excuses! / Don't make any excuses. / Don't give me excuses.

Useful Expressions 活學活用

聆聽英文內容

 情境一：不要忘記做功課

1. Did you get your homework done?
   你把功課做完了嗎？

2. When's your homework due?
   你的功課在什麼時候交？

3. I haven't finished my homework yet.
   我還沒有完成我的功課。

4. I will do my homework first and then play.
   我會先把功課做好才去玩耍。

 情境二：不專心時

5. I'll do my homework after playing for a little while.
   我先玩一會再做功課。

6. Pay attention.
   專心一點。

7. I'd like you to get your homework done without a hassle. 麻煩
   我希望你不要煩了，好好把功課完成吧。

家長手記

家長不要在子女面前比較，例如不要說出這樣的話：
Why can't you be more like your sister? She does her work without a hassle. （你就不能像你姐姐一樣嗎？她做功課可不會煩。）父母不必要的比較，鼓吹了孩子之間「競爭」的心態，使孩子的衝突及差異加劇。

 情境三：訂立規則

8. No video games or TV until my homework is done.
   功課還未做好以前，我不會玩遊戲和看電視。

9. When your homework is finished, then you can play.
   你做完功課以後就可以去玩耍。

Scene 20

檢查功課

I don't understand this one.
我不懂這一題。

💬 Conversation 美國家庭這樣説

Girl:　Mom, I don't understand this one.

Mom:　Let me help you.

Girl:　What does "MM/DD/YY" mean?

Mom:　That means Month/Day/Year. Use numbers.

Girl:　I don't understand.

Mom:　For example, if your birth date is May 4, 2017, write 05/04/17.

Girl:　Oh, I see.

英文能力 UP！

Oh, I see. 常見於英語口語，指「我明白了。」包含了在別人指點下恍然大悟的意思。很多人把 I see 説成 I know，但這是不恰當的。I know 指「我知道的」，言外之意是「不必你來告訴我」。

Useful Expressions 活學活用

聆聽英文內容

 ## 情境一：檢查作業

1. Are you having problems with your homework?

   你做功課有不明白的地方嗎？

2. I found three errors on this page. Can you find them?

   我在這頁看到三個錯處，你能找出來嗎？

 ## 情境二：提出疑問

3. I don't know how to do it.

   我不懂怎樣做。

4. Can you explain it to me?

   可以給我解釋一下嗎？

5. This is too difficult / easy.

   這太難 / 容易了。

6. No, Sweetie. It's easy if you know the way.

   不難的，小甜心。如果知道方法，就很簡單了。

家長手記

孩子做功課的時候，家長必須多作鼓勵，盡量避免說出如 You're so stupid / hopeless.（你真蠢 / 你是沒希望的了。）這樣羞辱的話。

 ## 情境三：進度良好

7. Good / Get going / Right / That's wonderful.

   做得好 / 繼續吧 / 做得對 / 非常好。

8. I can finish all my homework by myself.

   我能夠自己完成所有功課。

 ## 情境四：給予讚賞

9. I really like how you worked hard on your homework tonight! And you did it all by yourself! I am very proud of you!

   你今晚很用心做功課，我非常高興！而且你能自己完成所有功課，我為你感到驕傲！

Scene 21

收拾書包

Pack your school bag for tomorrow.

把明天的書包整理好。

💬 Conversation 美國家庭這樣說

Mom: Pack your school bag for tomorrow.

Boy: I was just about to pack my school bag. Mom, where's my weekly schedule?

Mom: It's on your desk.

Boy: Okay. Let me check if everything is here. I'm done packing, Mom.

Mom: Your school bag still looks heavy. You need to take everything out that you don't need.

英文能力 UP！

was about to do 表示「正準備做某事」，例如：I was just about to call you.（我正準備打電話給你。）

Useful Expressions 活學活用

聆聽英文內容

 情境一：整理書包

1. Did you pack your school bag?

   你整理好書包了嗎？

2. Pack your school bag before you go to sleep.

   睡覺前，先整理好書包。

3. I am going to pack my school bag.

   我正打算整理書包。

4. I finished packing my school bag.

   我整理好書包了。

 情境二：找齊需要的東西

5. Mom, where's my English book?

   媽，我的英文課本在哪裏？

6. I can't find my English exercise book.

   我找不到英文練習簿。

 情境三：再來檢查一次

7. Check if you have everything.

   檢查一下是不是都帶齊了。

8. Let me check if everything is okay.

   讓我檢查是不是都帶齊了。

9. I forgot to sharpen my pencils.

   我忘了削鉛筆。

10. Is my bag still heavy?

   我的書包還是很重嗎？

11. Take everything out that you don't need.

   把你不需要的東西都拿出來。

Scene 22

愉快的校園

How was school today?
今天在學校過得怎麼樣？

💬 Conversation 美國家庭這樣說

Mom: Sweetie, how was school today?

Boy: It was fine.

Mom: Did you have a good time with your friends?

Boy: Yes. We played ball games together.

Mom: That's good. Tell me one thing that you learned today.

Boy: I learned a new song today.

Mom: What song is that? Can you sing the song you learned?

Boy: Okay.

家長手記 問問孩子今天在學校有沒有發生什麼有趣的事情，會讓孩子感到被關心的溫暖呀！美國家長一般會說 How was school today?（今天在學校過得怎麼樣？）如果孩子去了露營或是郊遊玩樂，家長就可以問：Did you have a good time?（今天過得愉快嗎？）

Useful Expressions 活學活用

聆聽英文內容

 情境一：上學的感想

1. Was school fun?

   學校有趣嗎？

2. Yeah, it was fun.

   嗯，很有趣。

3. It was great.

   很好。

 情境二：在學校做什麼？

4. What did you play in school?

   你在學校玩了什麼？

5. We played with clay.

   我們玩黏土。

6. We played with the blocks.

   我們玩積木。

 情境三：談談有趣的事情

7. Did anything funny happen today?

   有沒有發生有趣的事情呢？

8. What was the most fun?

   什麼最有趣？

9. Playing outside was the best.

   在戶外玩的時候最有趣了。

10. I made some friends.

    我結識了幾個朋友。

11. My teacher praised me today.

    今天老師稱讚我了。

Scene 23

不想上學去

I don't want to go to school.

我不想上學去。

⚡ Conversation 美國家庭這樣説

Boy: Mom, I don't want to go to school.

Mom: Hey Sweetie, what happened? Did anyone make you upset at school?

Boy: Katie hit me. I hate her.

Mom: Why did she do that? Did she say sorry?

Boy: No. I'm never going to talk to her again.

家長手記

孩子不想上學的原因可能有很多，是不想與家人分開，還是遇到什麼負面的事情？父母必須與孩子多作溝通，嘗試了解他們真正的想法。跟孩子聊天時，可多問問正面的經驗：Did anything happy happen today?（今天有什麼高興的事發生嗎？）如果孩子遇到困難，父母可以與他們一起想辦法：Is it better to...?（如果⋯⋯會不會好些？），引導孩子樂觀地看待事情，同時培養解決問題的能力。

Useful Expressions 活學活用

聆聽英文內容

 情境一：在學校過得不開心

1. Did something happen with your classmates?

   你跟同學發生了什麼事嗎？

2. Did your classmate make you upset?

   你的同學讓你不開心嗎？

3. I really don't like him / her.

   我真的討厭他 / 她。

4. I don't want to play with him / her anymore.

   我再也不要跟他 / 她玩了。

 情境二：追問原因

5. Why? What happened? Does anyone from your class pick on you?

   為什麼？發生了什麼事？班裏有人欺負你嗎？

6. They keep bullying / teasing me.

   他們一直在欺負 / 嘲笑我。

7. Since when did they do that?

   他們是從什麼時候開始這樣做？

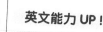

英文能力 UP！

Since when 用於口語中的問句，表示驚訝或氣憤。

8. From the start of the school year.

   從學期初開始。

 情境三：提出解決辦法

9. How about talking to him / her about your feelings?

   跟那些同學説説你的感受，怎麼樣？

10. Don't worry, Sweetie. Mom will help you. Let's talk to your teacher about it.

   小甜心，不要擔心。媽媽會幫你，我們把這事情告訴老師。

Scene 24

我的好朋友

She is your best friend, right?

她是你的好朋友，對嗎？

💬 Conversation 美國家庭這樣說

Mom: Sweetie, how many students are in your class?

Girl: There are twenty.

Mom: Who do you like most among your classmates?

Girl: I like Irina the most. She's really nice.

Mom: So Irina is your best friend, right? Is she sitting next to you?

Girl: No, but I always play with her during recess.

小息

英文能力 UP！

Among 指「在一個羣體之間」，among your classmates 就是指「在你的同學裏」。除了指人，也可以指事物，例如：I found my pen among the books on the desk.（我在書桌的書堆中找到了我的筆。）

Useful Expressions 活學活用

 情境一：誰是你的好朋友？

1. Do you have a best friend?
   你有好朋友嗎？

2. Yes, I have one best friend.
   有，我有一個好朋友。

3. Oh, what's his / her name?
   噢，他 / 她叫什麼名字？

4. Where does your best friend live?
   你的好朋友住在哪裏？

 情境二：最喜歡的好朋友

5. I like him / her the most. He / She is really nice.
   我最喜歡他 / 她，他 / 她真的很好。

6. He / She is such a good person. I want to get closer to him / her.
   他 / 她是個非常好的人，我想跟他 / 她做好朋友。

情境三：跟好朋友相處

7. I played with him / her during recess today.
   我今天在小息的時候跟他 / 她一起玩耍。

8. I want to go and play at his / her house.
   我想去他 / 她的家玩耍。

9. What games did you play?
   你們玩了些什麼呢？

10. What did you talk to him / her about today?
    你今天跟他 / 她聊了些什麼？

Scene 25

餐前洗手
Wash your hands first!
先去洗手！

Conversation 美國家庭這樣說

Mom:　Time for dinner!

Girl:　Wow, my favorite fried chicken drumstick!

Mom:　You haven't washed your hands yet!

Girl:　I'm so hungry. I can't wait a second longer. 　急不及待

Mom:　That doesn't mean you don't have to wash your hands first! Go! Remember to wash with soap to get rid of dirt and germs that could make us sick. 　清除

Girl:　All right.

英文能力 UP！

Can't wait 或 can hardly 常用於口語，用來強調説話者對即將發生的事急不及待或是感到興奮的心情。例如：The children can't wait for Christmas to come!（孩子等不及到聖誕節了。）又如：I can hardly wait to see you again!（我急不及待想再見到你！）

Useful Expressions 活學活用

聆聽英文內容

 ## 情境一：養成洗手的習慣

1. My hands are dirty.
   我的手髒了。

2. Go wash them right away.
   馬上去洗手。

3. How often do we have to wash our hands?
   我們應該隔多久洗手一次呢？

4. I wash my hands after I use the bathroom, when I'm preparing food, after I take out the trash, before I eat and every time I feel my hands have gotten dirty.
   我上廁所後會洗手，或準備食物時、處理垃圾後、吃東西前，總之每當我覺得手髒了，就會洗手。

 ## 情境二：洗手的步驟

5. Turn on the water. Wash for about 15 to 20 seconds.
   扭開水，洗 15 到 20 秒。

6. I wash my hands with soap.
   我用肥皂來洗手。

7. Work up some lather on both sides of your hands and between your fingers. Don't forget to wash around your nails. This is one place germs like to hide.
   擦出泡沫，洗擦手掌和手背，還有你的手指，不要忘了洗擦指甲四周，這裏最容易藏着污垢。

8. Rinse or dry well with a clean towel.
   沖洗乾淨，或用清潔的毛巾擦乾手。

西方文化 GoGoGo!

為了讓孩子更好地記得搓肥皂的時間，美國家長或老師一般會讓孩子唱一遍 ABC 字母歌或兩次生日歌，唱完剛好是 20 秒左右。孩子通過歌聲記住了洗手的時間，保證把手洗得乾乾淨淨。

Scene 26

吃早餐

Breakfast is ready.

早餐已經準備好了。

💬 Conversation 美國家庭這樣説

Mom: <mark>Come along</mark>, everybody. Breakfast is ready.

Girl: Mom, what do we have for breakfast this morning?

Mom: I've made some cereal and scrambled eggs for all of us.

Girl: I like that. Can I have some toast as well?

Mom: Of course. Do you want some butter for your toast?

Girl: Yes, please. And lots of jam as well.

英文能力 UP！

Come along! 屬命令句式，用來催促別人趕快做某事，例如：Come along!
We're all waiting for you! （快點！我們都在等着你！）又如：Come along!
We're late. （快點！我們遲到了。）

Useful Expressions 活學活用

聆聽英文內容

 情境一：要吃早餐了

1. It's time for breakfast.

   是時候吃早餐了。

2. Breakfast is on the table.

   早餐已放在餐桌上了。

 情境二：早餐吃什麼？

3. What do you want to eat for breakfast?

   你早餐想要吃些什麼？

4. I just want some toast and OJ.

   我只想吃吐司和橙汁。

5. I want some cereal for breakfast.

   我早餐想吃穀類食物。

6. I like to eat bread.

   我喜歡吃麵包。

7. Oatmeal and toast sounds good to me.

   我覺得燕麥片粥和吐司很不錯。

英文能力 UP！

OJ 是 orange juice 的簡稱，常用於口語。

英文能力 UP！

在美國，oatmeal 主要指燕麥片粥。英國人說 oatmeal 時，一般指燕麥片和燕麥粉。

 情境三：讓孩子試試塗吐司

8. How do you like your toast?

   你要在吐司上塗什麼？

9. I want some strawberry jam for my bread.

   我要在麵包上塗些草莓醬。

10. Spread it evenly.

    要均勻地塗。

11. Let me try.

    我來試試看。

Scene 27

吃零食

I want my chocolate!

我要吃巧克力！

💬 Conversation 美國家庭這樣說

Mom: What are you doing? You don't eat chocolate without asking!?

Boy: Yum-yum. Yum-yum.

Mom: You can't have it anymore.

Boy: I want my chocolate!

Mom: You know, you had two giant scoops of ice cream already today! Let's have chocolate another night.

英文能力 UP！

在口語中，人們常用 yum-yum 或 yummy 來誇讚食物好吃。此外，人們還用以下方式來表示食物美味。例如：It's delicious / tasty.（太好吃了。）/ Wow, it tastes so good!（嘩，這太好吃了！）/ I've never tasted anything better.（我從沒吃過比這個更好吃的東西。）/ I'm drooling.（我要流口水了。）

Useful Expressions 活學活用

聆聽英文內容

 情境一：吃零食或甜品

1. Mom, I want to eat a snack with you.
   媽，我想和您一起吃零食。

2. OK. Wash your hands first, then we can have some dessert.
   好的，先去洗手，然後我們吃甜品。

 情境二：孩子想多吃一點

3. Can I have more cookies?
   我可以多吃一點甜餅乾嗎？

4. Let's have cookies for a snack next week. Good idea!
   好主意！我們下星期就吃甜餅乾吧。

5. Can I have one more piece of cake, Mom?
   媽，我可以多吃一塊蛋糕嗎？

6. We usually have cake at birthday parties. The next one is Irina's birthday party which is coming soon.
   我們一般在生日會上才吃蛋糕。下次是艾雲娜的生日派對，很快就來到啦。

 情境三：吃零食與甜品要適可而止

7. No more today!
   今天不能再吃了！

8. The last piece is for your dessert. We're having dinner soon.
   把最後一件留作飯後甜品，我們很快就吃晚餐了。

9. We had something sweet already today. Let's have chocolate another night.
   我們今天已經吃了甜品，過幾個晚上我們才吃巧克力吧。

10. No more candy. My teeth are going to fall out!
    不能再吃糖果，我的牙齒要掉了！

Scene 28 吃晚餐

Dinner's almost ready.
晚餐快準備好了。

 Conversation 美國家庭這樣說

Mom: Dinner's almost ready, we'll be eating in fifteen minutes. Sweetie, please come to the table now. Can you also tell Daddy that dinner's ready?

Girl: Yes.

Mom: Can you also help me set the table? 擺餐具

Girl: OK. I'll place the silverware on the table.

Mom: Great! Remember that on the left of the plate is the fork, and on the right are the knife and spoon.

西方文化 GoGoGo!

在美國，人們進餐時會保持着左叉右刀的姿勢，右手持刀切食物，左手持叉吃東西。刀叉是自然成對的名詞，「一副刀叉」的英文是 a knife and fork。

Useful Expressions 活學活用

聆聽英文內容

 情境一：吃晚飯了

1. Dinner is ready! Come and eat your dinner.
   晚餐準備好了！過來吃晚餐吧。

2. I made your favorite.
   我做了你最喜歡吃的菜。

3. I'm coming, Mom.
   媽，我來啦。

4. Mom, I'll help set the table.
   媽，我幫您擺餐具。

 情境二：給孩子心理準備

5. Put away your toys, it's time for dinner.
   把你的玩具收拾好，是時候吃晚餐了。

6. Clear your stuff off the table, dinner's almost ready.
   把你的東西拿走，收拾好桌子，晚餐快準備好了。

7. You can watch TV for a little while, but just so you know, we'll be eating dinner very soon.
   你可以再看一會兒電視，但必須知道我們馬上要吃晚餐了。

 **家長手記**

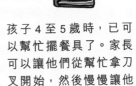

孩子 4 至 5 歲時，已可以幫忙擺餐具了。家長可以讓他們從幫忙拿刀叉開始，然後慢慢讓他們幫忙擺盤子。

 情境三：互相讚美

8. Thank you for coming so quickly.
   謝謝你這麼快就過來了。

9. Hmm, that smells so good.
   嗯，味道很香。

10. Mommy's food is the best.
    媽媽做的菜是最好的。

11. Mom, thank you for the food.
    媽，謝謝您準備晚餐。

Scene 29

不偏吃
Clean your plate!
吃光碟子上的食物！

💬 Conversation 美國家庭這樣說

Mom: Can you eat everything on your plate? Food is for eating, not for playing. Eat all of your dinner!

Boy: I'm full.

Mom: No. You didn't eat enough. Clean your plate.

Boy: Yuck! I don't want that.

Mom: You certainly are picky! If you don't eat all of this, you can't have ice cream.

英文能力 UP！

I'm full. 的意思是吃飽了，此外可以用 stuffed 這個詞語。如果有人問：
Would you like another piece of pizza？（再來一塊薄餅吧？）就可以回答：
No, thanks. I'm stuffed.（不，謝謝，我吃飽了。）

Useful Expressions 活學活用

聆聽英文內容

 情境一：偏吃的藉口

1. Mom, I don't like it.
   媽，我不喜歡這個。

2. It's getting cold.
   （食物）已經放涼了。

 情境二：幫助孩子改掉偏吃的習慣

3. Don't be so picky about food.
   不要偏吃。

4. Can you eat everything on your plate?
   你可以把碟子上的食物吃掉嗎？

 情境三：每種食物都有好處

5. This fish will help your bones get stronger.
   這條魚可以讓你的骨頭更強健。

6. It's good for my body.
   這個對我的身體好。

7. I will get taller if I eat this.
   我吃了這個便會長高。

西方文化 GoGoGo!

美國的家長決不讓孩子成為偏吃的人（picky eater / fussy eater），他們不僅給孩子講解每道菜的營養、味道，還會以身作則，改變孩子任性、自私的習慣。

 情境四：孩子還是不肯吃時

8. I see you're not eating your chicken. Mind if I give it to your brother / sister?
   你不吃雞肉的話，那我給兄弟 / 姐妹吃了，好嗎？

9. Eat all of your dinner! There are starving children in Africa who would love to have that as a meal!
   要把飯吃光！非洲那些飢餓的孩子多麼想吃到這麼一頓飯呀！

Scene 30

餐桌禮儀

Don't talk with food in your mouth.

不要在吃東西的時候説話。

💬 Conversation 美國家庭這樣説

Girl: Bmdoyonowoormobooo…

Mom: Sorry, I can't understand you with your mouth full of food.

Girl: I said, do you know where my Barbie doll is?

Mom: Okay. Don't talk with food in your mouth. It's hard to hear what you want to say, since you're chewing the words together with the food.

Girl: I'm sorry.

西方文化 GoGoGo!

在美國，孩子的禮儀教育始於餐桌。自孩子上餐桌的第一天起，家長便開始對他們進行「進餐教育」（table manners training）。

Useful Expressions 活學活用

聆聽英文內容

 情境一：孩子不願吃飯的話

1. I don't want to eat, Mommy.

   媽媽，我不想吃。

2. I'm not hungry.

   我不餓。

3. You don't have to eat, but family dinners are about being with family, and not just eating. So we all have to sit at the table.

   你不一定要吃，不過吃晚餐的意義是跟家人在一起，不單單是吃東西，所以我們還是要坐在一起。

 情境二：訂立吃飯時的規矩

4. Sit properly when eating.

   吃飯時要坐好。

5. No television during meals.

   吃飯時不能看電視。

6. Keep your elbows off the table.

   手肘不要靠在桌上。

7. Keep your mouth closed when chewing.

   閉着嘴巴咀嚼食物。

情境三：學會了餐桌禮儀

8. I won't talk with my mouth full of food.

   我不會在吃東西時説話。

9. I won't slurp my drink / soup.

   我喝飲料 / 湯時不會發出咕嚕咕嚕的聲響。

10. I won't play with my food.

   我不會拿食物來玩。

Scene 31 外出用餐

Let's eat out tonight.
我們今晚去外面吃吧。

💬 Conversation 美國家庭這樣說

Mom: At the restaurant the waiters are rushing around balancing trays of food. How can we help them do a good job and not spill things?

Boy: No running around.

Mom: You're right! When you're in a restaurant, you must walk.

Boy: But what if I'm in a hurry? Why can't I run if I want to?

Mom: Because it's against the rule to run in a restaurant. Running is for outside where you have lots of room to run.

家長手記

孩子說對了話，家長可以稱讚他們：You're right.（你說得對。）其他相近意思的說法還有：Well said.（說得好。）/ You got it.（你說對了。）/ That's for sure.（那是當然。）/ That's true.（正是如此。）

Useful Expressions 活學活用

聆聽英文內容

 情境一：外出用餐

1. Let's eat out.
   我們去外面吃吧。

2. Hurray! I want to.
   太好了！我要去。

3. What do you want to eat?
   你想吃什麼呢？

4. How about pizza, Mom?
   媽，吃薄餅好嗎？

 情境二：外出時也要注意餐桌禮儀

5. Where should I put this napkin, Mom?
   媽，這餐巾該放在哪裏？

6. Place the napkin in your lap.
   把餐巾放在大腿上。

7. Sit still. Don't fidget at the table.
   坐好，用餐時不要左搖右擺。

8. Be careful not to drop the food.
   小心不要把食物掉到地上。

西方文化 GoGoGo!

美國人平日好動，揮手聳肩等肢體語言（body language）十分豐富，但一旦上餐桌便專心致志地吃東西。這跟中國人圍着餐桌滔滔不絕談天的情況很不一樣。

 情境三：使用刀叉時要小心

9. I won't point my fork.
   我不會用叉指着別人。

10. Don't use your knife to put food in your mouth. That's dangerous!
    不要用刀來把食物放進口裏，這樣做很危險！

75

Scene 32

點餐

Are you ready to order?
你準備好點餐了嗎？

💬 Conversation 美國家庭這樣說

Waiter: Here are your menus. Today's special is grilled salmon.
I'll be back to take your order in a minute.

Waiter: Are you ready to order?

Mom:　I'd like the seafood spaghetti.

Waiter: And you?

Boy:　 I'll have grilled chicken with potatoes.

Waiter: Would you like anything to drink?

Boy:　 I'll have a cola, please.

英文能力 UP！

Would you 聽上去比 Do you 更有禮貌，尤其對不熟悉的人，
或在餐廳裏點餐的場合使用。

Useful Expressions 活學活用

聆聽英文內容

 情境一：準備好點餐

1. We're ready to order.

   我們可以點餐了。

2. Would you like an appetizer?

   你需要前菜嗎？

情境二：學習怎樣點餐（前菜和主菜）

3. I'd like a bowl of vegetable soup, please.

   我想要一碗菜湯，謝謝。

4. I'd like to have the salad, please.

   我想要沙律（沙拉），謝謝。

5. I'd like a hamburger and fries.

   我想要漢堡包和炸薯條。

英文能力 UP！

Fries 是炸薯條的美式叫法，英式英語是 chips。

情境三：學習怎樣點餐（飲品和甜品）

6. I'd like a glass of orange juice, please.

   我想要一杯橙汁，謝謝。

7. I'll have some water, please.

   我想要水，謝謝。

8. I'd like a mango ice cream, please.

   我想要一份芒果冰淇淋，謝謝。

 情境四：吃飽了

9. How was everything?

   你覺得食物怎樣？

10. Delicious. Thanks.

   很好吃，謝謝。

西方文化 GoGoGo!

一般來説，正規的西餐包括了餐湯（soup）、前菜（appetizer）、主菜（main course）、飲品（drinks）和甜品（dessert）。

Scene 33

清潔地板

Can you get me the broom?
你能給我掃帚嗎？

💬 Conversation 美國家庭這樣說

Boy:　Mom, can you get me the broom? I'm gonna sweep the floor.

Mom:　Here you are. Do you know how to sweep the floor? Let me show you. You'll need to sweep the dirt into a pile, then sweep the dirt into the dustpan.

Boy:　Let me try. Mom, this isn't all clean yet.

Mom:　You'll have to make sure the broom reaches into the angle of each corner so that you sweep out the dust from there.

英文能力 UP！

在美式口語常會聽到 gonna 這個單詞，其實它是 going to 的口語形式，例如：I'm gonna call you later. 意思就是 I'm going to call you later.（我稍後給你打電話。）

Useful Expressions 活學活用

聆聽英文內容

 情境一：幫忙掃地

1. Can you help me sweep the floor, Sweetie?

   小甜心，你能幫我掃地嗎？

2. I'm going to sweep the floor now.

   我現在要掃地了。

情境二：用其他方式清潔地板

3. We need to use the vacuum.

   我們要用吸塵機來吸塵。

> **英文能力 UP！**
> 這是 vacuum cleaner（真空吸塵機）的縮寫。

4. Let's wipe the floor with a rag.

   我們用抹布來擦地板吧。

5. Can you get me the rag?

   你能幫我拿抹布嗎？

6. The rag's too dirty. We need to wash the rag.

   抹布太髒了，我們要洗一下抹布。

7. Turn the rag over and clean the floor.

   把抹布翻過來，然後清潔地板。

 情境三：打掃的苦與樂

8. Is it all clean now? Wiping the floor is tiring.

   都清潔好了嗎？擦地很辛苦呀。

9. My knees hurt after kneeling down.

   跪在地上，膝蓋好痛呀。

10. You did a great job sweeping the floor. Well done!

    你把地板掃得很乾淨，做得很好！

11. Thank you for helping me clean up this mess.　打掃

    謝謝你幫忙把這麼亂的地方打掃好。

Scene 34

收拾房間

Let's clean your room!

我們來收拾一下你的房間吧！

💬 Conversation 美國家庭這樣説

Mom: It's almost time to clean up.

Boy: No, Mommy. I am playing with Anna.

Mom: I need you to clean up your room first, okay?

Boy: But I really want to play with Anna.

Mom: Why yes, you certainly can do that… as soon as you tidy up your room. Go put your books away and make your bed.

Boy: OK.

家長手記

如家長需要向孩子傳達明確的要求，就可以用 I need you to... 的句式。例如：I need you to put away your books now. Is that clear?（我要你馬上把書本收拾好，清楚了嗎？）

Useful Expressions 活學活用

聆聽英文內容

 情境一：是時候收拾一下

1. Your room is in such a mess.
   你的房間太亂了。

2. The bookshelves are all messed up.
   書架已經亂得不像樣了。

3. I'm sorry. I'll clean it up right away.
   不好意思，我現在馬上打掃。

4. I won't mess it up next time.
   我不會再把地方弄得這麼亂了。

 情境二：待會再收拾

5. Can I play a little longer?
   我可以再玩一會（才收拾）嗎？

6. I'll clean up after a little while.
   我等一下會收拾的。

 情境三：作適當的誘導

7. Please clear off your desk.
   請把書桌清理乾淨。

8. Put your books away.
   把你的書本收拾好。

家長手記

稱讚（praise）是用來鼓勵孩子的方式，家長還要經常告訴孩子，對他們的幫助多麼感激。這種真誠的感謝會令孩子更積極地做家務。

 情境四：多作讚美

9. You did a great job cleaning up the place.
   做得很好，你把整個地方打掃好了。

10. Thanks for helping tidy up the room, that made a big difference!
    謝謝你幫忙把房間收拾整齊，現在變得煥然一新了！

Scene 35

整理牀鋪

Remember to make your bed.
記住把你的牀鋪整理好。

💬 Conversation 美國家庭這樣說

Mom: Your bed is so messy! Before you leave for school, please remember to make your bed.

Girl: What's the big deal about having to make my bed anyway? Did you make your own bed when you were a little girl?

Mom: Making my own bed was a habit I learned from my Mom. This is the same habit I want you to have. There was no excuse for me not to do it. I want you to understand that you're responsible for the bed you sleep on, too.

英文能力 UP！

英語口語中常聽到這麼一句話：It's not a big deal.（沒什麼大不了的。）它用來表達不過如此的意思，或安慰他人沒什麼大不了。

Useful Expressions 活學活用

聆聽英文內容

 情境一：整理牀鋪

1. Let's make your bed.
   我們來整理一下你的牀鋪吧。

2. Let me put away my stuffed animals.
   我來把毛絨動物娃娃收拾好。

3. I can pull up the covers.
   我來拉開被子。

4. Let's change the sheets.
   我們來換牀單吧。

 情境二：收拾好了

5. It's done, Mom.
   媽，完成了。

6. Marvelous!
   太好了！

前美國軍官指出，如果每天早上整理牀鋪，相當於完成當天第一個任務，這會帶來小小的成就感（sense of achievement），激勵人執行一個又一個任務。

 情境三：養成好習慣

7. Making your bed is a simple habit.
   整理牀鋪是簡單的生活習慣。

8. A tidy bed will make your room look great.
   一張整齊的牀會讓你的房間看起來很棒。

9. I love coming into my room and seeing the bed made. It's so neat and tidy!
   我喜歡走進自己的房間時看到牀鋪已經整理好，真是乾淨又整齊！

10. I won't leave my bed messy again.
    我不會再讓我的牀變得凌亂了。

Scene 36

收拾玩具
Clean up your toys!
把你的玩具收拾好！

💬 Conversation 美國家庭這樣說

Mom: Let's all pitch in. Let's start by putting away whatever is small enough to fit in the palm of your hand, okay?

Boy: This robot is very small.

Mom: Right. Do you want to put it on the shelf?

Boy: Hmm.

Mom: Now, let's put away anything with red on it.

Boy: This car is red. Let's put it in the box.

Mom: Good.

英文能力 UP！

Pitch in 是非正式用語，多用於口語中，有「齊心合力把事情做好」的意思，
例如：If we all pitch in, we'll have it finished in no time.（我們大家合力的話，
很快就可以完成了。）

84

Useful Expressions 活學活用

聆聽英文內容

 情境一：收拾玩具

1. Tidy up your toys.
   收拾好你的玩具。

2. I was just about to clean that up.
   我正打算要整理。

3. I'll put my toys away.
   我會把玩具收拾好。

4. Think about where you should store your toys so they're in a safe place. Come and tell me when you've decided on a good spot.
   想想你的玩具應放在哪個安全的地方，想好了就過來告訴我。

 情境二：孩子不聽話時

5. As soon as your toys are put away, we get to go to the park.
   你要先把玩具收拾好，我們才去公園。

6. We can't have dessert until your toys are put away.
   要是你不把玩具收拾好，我們就不能吃甜品。

7. If you do not clean up your toys by the time the timer goes off, I'm going to put them in the store room until Saturday.
   如果計時器的時間到了你還沒有把玩具收拾好的話，那麼我就把玩具放進儲物室，星期六前都不能再拿出來。

8. Sorry, I'm not done playing.
   對不起，我還在玩。

 情境三：讚美乖孩子

9. I like the way you remembered to pack up your toys.
   看到你記得把玩具收拾好，我真高興。

處理垃圾

I want you to take out the garbage.
我想你把垃圾拿到外面。

💬 Conversation 美國家庭這樣說

Mom: Grandma and Grandpa are coming to visit tomorrow and I need you to help me with some chores. Have you swept and mopped the kitchen floor?

Boy: Yes.

Mom: Now I want you to take out the garbage, okay?

Boy: Okay. Should I put this pile of old newspapers into the recycle bin?

Mom: Sure! You're such a good boy.

英文能力 UP！

美國人一般把「垃圾」叫作 garbage 或 trash，英國人則叫 rubbish。而「垃圾工人」和「清潔工人」的美式叫法是 garbage man、garbage collector 或 trash man，在英國則叫 dustman 或 dustbin man。「垃圾車」在美國叫 garbage truck，在英國則叫 dustcart。

Useful Expressions 活學活用

 情境一：幫忙清理垃圾

1. Let me put the newspapers in the recycle bin.
   我來把報紙放進回收箱吧。

2. I'll empty the wastepaper baskets.
   我會清理一下廢紙箱。

> **英文能力 UP！**
> 英式英語會説成：Can you put out the bins?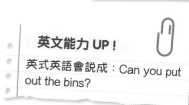

3. I'll put away the bins.
   我會把垃圾箱收拾好。

4. Can you take out the garbage / trash?
   你可以把垃圾拿到外面嗎？

 情境二：哪些廢物可以循環再造？

5. Do you know that most of our trash can be recycled?
   你知道大部分垃圾都可以循環再造的嗎？

6. I know paper can be recycled.
   我知道紙張可以循環再造。

7. Plastic, glass, metal, batteries and textiles can be recycled, too.
   塑料、玻璃、金屬、電池和紡織品都可以循環再造。

 情境三：循環再造的好處

8. Every time we recycle, we save our environment a little more.
   我們每次把垃圾循環再造，就可以為保護環境出一分力。

9. We cut down fewer trees, and use less water and energy.
   我們砍少了樹，用少了水，也用少了能源。

10. When we recycle, a new product can be made out of it, and it will be useful again!
    當我們循環再造，就能從中製造出新產品，讓垃圾再次變得有用！

Scene 38 整理衣物

Let's fold these clothes neatly.
我們來把這些衣物摺好。

💬 Conversation 美國家庭這樣説

Mom:　The clothes are all dry. Let's take them off the racks.

Girl:　OK. Whose is this?

Mom:　That's Daddy's. Let's fold these clothes neatly.

Girl:　Let me fold mine by myself.

Mom:　OK. Fold it in half like this.

Girl:　Did I do a good job folding these clothes?

Mom:　Well done, Sweetie. Can you now put the clothes away
　　　　where they belong?

英文能力 UP！

Do a good job 是「事情做得很好」的意思。Good 還可以用 fine、great、
excellent 等單詞取代，意思一樣。當然，如果將 good 改用 bad 或 poor，
就是指「事情做得不好」了。

Useful Expressions 活學活用

聆聽英文內容

情境一：整理好衣服

1. Mom, let me fold my own clothes.

   媽，我來摺自己的衣服吧。

2. This is how you fold clothes.

   你要像這樣摺衣服。

3. Fold them neatly.

   摺整齊一點。

4. This is too big for me to fold.

   這件衣服太大，我摺不了。

5. I will put them in the drawer.

   我會把它們放在抽屜裏。

6. Let me hang my own coat / jacket up.

   我來把自己的外套掛好。

情境二：處理髒衣服

7. These socks smell bad!

   這些襪子好臭！

8. Mom, should my school uniform be washed?

   媽，我的校服要洗嗎？

9. Put these dirty clothes into the basket / hamper.

   把這些髒衣服放進籃子裏。

10. Let's do the laundry.

    我們來洗衣服吧。

11. Dirty clothes go in the laundry basket. We don't wear them until they're back in the drawer.

    髒衣服要放進洗衣籃裏，等洗好放回抽屜後，我們就可以再穿了。

Scene 39

親子廚房

Would you like to be my little helper?
你要當我的小助手嗎？

💬 Conversation 美國家庭這樣說

Girl:　Mom, what's for a snack?

Mom:　I'm going to make some chocolate chip cookies.

Girl:　Wow! That's my favorite.

Mom:　Would you like to be my little helper? You are so good at mixing the ingredients.

Girl:　Sure. I'll help you bake the cookies as well.

Mom:　Good girl.

英文能力 UP！

Wow! 是最常用來表達驚訝的感歎詞，除了 Wow! 之外，英語中還有許多其他表達驚訝的詞語，例如：Oh!（噢！）/ What?（什麼？）/ Whoa!（哇！）/ Really?（真的嗎？）

Useful Expressions 活學活用

聆聽英文內容

 情境一：幫忙準備材料

1. I'm going to make dinner now. Can you be my little helper?

   我準備做晚餐了，你可以做我的小助手嗎？

2. I can peel the potatoes.

   我可以把馬鈴薯削皮。

3. I can chop this carrot.

   我可以把這紅蘿蔔切件。

4. I can wash the fruit and veggies.

   我可以清洗水果和蔬菜。

5. Use a spoon to mix the ingredients together.

   用勺子把材料混合在一起。

> **英文能力 UP！**
> Veggies 是 vegetables 的美式說法。

 情境二：幫忙煮食

6. Mom, the water is boiling.

   媽，水煮沸了。

7. Let's turn down the stove.

   來把瓦斯爐調成小火吧。

 情境三：要注意安全

8. Can I cut it, Mom?

   媽，我能切它嗎？

9. Be careful with the knife.

   小心使用刀。

10. Don't try to catch a falling knife.

    不要接住掉下的刀。

11. Don't walk around while holding the scissors.

    不要拿着剪刀到處走。

西方文化 GoGoGo！

廚房在許多家長眼裏是孩子的禁區，但近年「廚房教育」（kitchen training）卻在美國流行起來。專家認為在保障安全的情況下，讓孩子走進廚房，不僅可以培養孩子的自理能力，還可以增進親子關係。

Scene 40

照顧弟妹

I'm a big brother now.

我現在是哥哥了。

💬 Conversation 美國家庭這樣說

Mom: Sweetie, look at who's here! This is our new little baby!

Boy: Wow, I'm a big brother now.

Mom: How do you feel about having a baby sister now?

Boy: I'm really happy to have her. She looks like a pretty doll.

Mom: Good. I'm so happy you love your sister so much. Do you want to sing her a lullaby?

西方文化 GoGoGo!

在西方國家，lullaby（搖籃曲，又稱催眠曲）的歷史源遠流長。搖籃曲通常都很簡短，而且旋律輕柔甜美，是美國父母常用來哄寶寶入睡的歌曲。

Useful Expressions 活學活用

聆聽英文內容

 情境一：幫忙照顧弟妹

1. I want to give my brother / sister a hug.
   我想抱抱弟弟 / 妹妹。

2. Hug her gently.
   輕輕的抱。

3. Can you help put the milk powder into the bottle?
   你可以幫忙把奶粉倒進奶瓶嗎？

4. Can you sing him / her a song?
   你可以給他 / 她唱首歌嗎？

 情境二：孩子吃醋了

5. I don't like my baby brother / sister.
   我討厭弟弟 / 妹妹。

6. Why don't you like him / her?
   你為什麼討厭他 / 她？

7. He / She just keeps crying all the time.
   他 / 她一直在哭。

8. He / She bothers me too much.
   他 / 她太麻煩了。

家長手記

孩子做錯事時，家長不要說些恐嚇的話，如「我疼妹妹，不疼你了。」這樣會令他們對弟妹產生敵意。

 情境三：做個好哥哥或好姐姐

9. I'll get along well with my baby brother / sister.
   我會跟弟弟 / 妹妹好好相處的。

10. You should love your brother / sister.
    你應該愛你的弟弟 / 妹妹。

11. I really like the gentle way you played with your baby sister.
    我很高興你這樣細心地跟弟弟 / 妹妹玩。

Scene 41

看電視

What's on TV now?

現在播放什麼電視節目？

💬 Conversation 美國家庭這樣説

Boy:　Mom, I want to watch TV. What's on TV now?

Mom:　Well, you may watch a cartoon now.

Boy:　I love it.

Mom:　I'll set the timer for one hour. When the timer goes off, we'll stop. Okay?

Boy:　I want to watch for two hours.

Mom:　Two hours is too long. Let's watch for only one hour.

英文能力 UP！

on 用於廣播或電視的場合裏，有「播放」的意思，例如：What's on TV tonight?（今晚播放什麼電視節目？）又如：What's on at the movies?（電影院在上映什麼電影？）

Useful Expressions 活學活用

聆聽英文內容

 情境一：看電視

1. Mom, can I watch TV?

   媽，我可以看電視嗎？

2. All right.

   好的。

3. Is there anything interesting on TV?

   有什麼好看的節目嗎？

4. What's on Channel Two?

   第二頻道在播什麼？

西方文化 GoGoGo!

美國兒科學會建議 2 歲以上孩子每天看電視不得超過 2 小時，而且只看優質兒童節目，如美國最受歡迎的教育節目《芝麻街》（*Sesame Street*）。

 情境二：訂下規則

5. Let's set up a time to watch TV. It's not good to watch too much TV.

   我們訂下看電視的時間吧，電視看得太多是不好的。

6. Back off a little.The TV will hurt your eyes.

   往後一點，電視會損害你的眼睛。

 情境三：看完電視了

7. No more today, honey. It's your reading time now.

   寶貝，今天看夠了。現在該是閱讀的時間了。

8. It's finished. Let me turn off the TV.

   播完了，我來把電視關掉。

9. I don't want to watch TV anymore.

   我不想再看電視了。

10.I can see why you like this show – it's really funny!

   我知道你為什麼喜歡看這個節目，真的很有趣！

Scene 42

玩遊戲

Are you ready to have fun?

你準備好一起玩了嗎？

💬 Conversation 美國家庭這樣說

Mom: Are you ready to have fun?

Girl: Yes, Mom, I'm bored. Can you play with me?

Mom: Okay, let's find something fun. What do you want to do with me, Sweetie?

Girl: Hide and seek!

Mom: Okay. I'll be "it", so you hide. Hmm, where' s my little girl? I can't see you. Where did you go? I can hear you now! Are you hiding under the desk? Yay, I got you!

家長手記　在與孩子互動的過程中，家長最常用的一句話就是 Are you ready?（你準備好了嗎？）例如：Are you ready to have fun? / Are you ready to go? / Are you ready for the exam? 孩子準備好了的話，家長可以教他們回答：Yes, I'm ready.（是的，準備好了。）

Useful Expressions 活學活用

聆聽英文內容

 情境一：一起玩遊戲

1. I hate to play alone.
   我討厭一個人玩。

2. Mom, I love it when you play games with me.
   媽，我喜歡您跟我一起玩遊戲。

3. Playing with my sweetie is the most fun.
   跟我的小甜心玩是最有趣。

 情境二：不同的互動遊戲

4. Let's solve a puzzle.
   我們來玩拼圖吧。

5. Let's play rock, paper, scissors.
   我們來玩剪刀石頭布吧。

6. I like to play hide and seek.
   我想玩捉迷藏。

7. I want to play doctor.
   我想玩扮醫生遊戲。

> **英文能力 UP！**
>
> 「剪刀石頭布」換成英語的話，除了次序變成 rock, paper, scissors 之外，當中的「布」還變成「紙」。在香港，這遊戲稱為「包剪揼」。

 情境三：想繼續玩下去

8. Mom, I want to play more.
   媽，我要繼續玩下去。

9. Just one more round, please?
   讓我再多玩一回好嗎？

10. That was fun. Want to do it again?
    真好玩，要再來一次嗎？

11. Mom's tired. Ask Daddy to play with you.
    媽媽累了，叫爸爸跟你玩吧。

Scene 43

親子閱讀

I want to read a book with you.

我們一起看看書。

💬 **Conversation 美國家庭這樣說**

Mom: Sweetie, I want to read a book with you. Which book should we read – this one or that one?

Girl: What is this one about?

Mom: This is a story about a special friendship between a boy and a dog. I have read this many times. I wonder what you will think about it.

Girl: And that one?

Mom: That is a story of a boy who goes on a very unusual trip. I chose it because we just came back from a trip.

Girl: I want that one.

Useful Expressions 活學活用

聆聽英文內容

 情境一：認識要看的書

1. What is the title?

   書名是什麼？

2. I like the cover of the book.

   我喜歡這本書的封面。

3. What is this story about?

   這是一個怎麼樣的故事？

 情境二：啟發孩子的想像力

4. What do you think will happen on the next page?

   你認為下一頁會發生什麼呢？

5. What makes you think that?

   為什麼你會這樣想？

6. Well, that's an interesting idea. How did you think of that?

   嗯，這個想法很有意思。你是怎樣想出來的呢？

7. That's one possibility. Let's see what the author has in mind.

   這也有可能，我們來看看作者是怎麼想的。

 情境三：讀完這本書了

西方文化 GoGoGo!

8. Do you like the story? Why (not)?

   你喜歡這故事嗎？為什麼（不）？

9. Who's your favorite character? Why?

   你最喜歡的角色是誰？為什麼？

10. It was fun / sad.

   故事很有趣 / 傷感。

11. Mom, read it again, please!

   媽，請再讀一次！

美國紐約市教育局最近成立了 Afterschool Reading Club（課後閱讀俱樂部），讓孩子可以在課外時間與家長共同閱讀書籍，更大力提倡「閱讀是沒有假期的」。

Scene 44

使用電腦

Mom, can I play computer games?
媽，我可以玩電腦遊戲嗎？

💬 Conversation 美國家庭這樣說

Boy:　Mom, can I play computer games?

Mom:　My sweetie **must have been** bored. Well, you can play after you do your homework.

Boy:　I'm done with my homework already.

Mom:　Okay. Then you can play.

Boy:　Yeah! I need to win this time.

英文能力 UP！

must have been 是對過去可能的猜測，表示某人或某事物必定已經做了怎樣的事情。例如：The streets are wet. It must have rained last night. （街道都濕了，昨晚一定下過雨。）

Useful Expressions 活學活用

聆聽英文內容

 情境一：玩電腦遊戲的感想

1. I like playing computer / online games.
   我喜歡玩電腦 / 網絡遊戲。

2. When I play, an hour feels like a second.
   我玩的時候，一個小時就像一秒般過去。

3. This game is fun.
   這個遊戲很好玩。

 情境二：訂立規則

4. You have to do your homework before you play.
   你玩之前一定要做好功課。

5. Let's make it a rule to play for only one hour.
   我們訂個規則，只能玩一個小時。

 情境三：時間到了

6. Mom, I want to play more.
   媽，我想再玩一下。

7. I'll be finished soon.
   我很快就玩完。

8. Enough with your computer games.
   Go do your homework now.
   電腦遊戲玩夠了，現在快點去做功課。

9. If you don't turn off your computer, then
   I won't allow you to play it again.
   如果你不把電腦關掉，我就不讓你再玩了。

10. Your eyesight will get bad when you play too much.
    玩太久的話，你的視力會變差的。

 西方文化 GoGoGo!

美國兒科學會認為，兒童應盡量少接觸任何電子媒體。因此美國家庭會跟孩子訂立 screen time（屏幕時間），以免他們患上近視（short-sightedness）。

Scene 45

唱歌和聽音樂

Mom, let's sing together.

媽，我們一起唱歌吧。

💬 Conversation 美國家庭這樣說

Girl:　Mom, let's sing together.

Mom:　Okay, what song shall we sing?

Girl:　Let's sing *Twinkle, Twinkle Little Star*.

Mom:　Do you want to sing the first verse, and Mom the second? 正歌

Girl:　Okay. Twinkle, twinkle, little star. How I wonder what you are...

Mom:　Wow, you look like an angel when you sing.

Twinkle, Twinkle, Little Star 是一首相當著名的西方兒歌，旋律來自法國古老民謠《媽媽請聽我說》。年輕的莫札特（Mozart）旅居巴黎時為這首民謠譜寫出鋼琴變奏曲。後來，變奏曲填上了詩人珍·泰勒（Jane Taylor）的英文詩《小星星》（*The Star*），成為現在廣為人知的《小星星變奏曲》。

Useful Expressions 活學活用

聆聽英文內容

 情境一：唱唱歌吧

1. Mom, listen to me sing.

   媽，聽我唱歌。

2. I like singing.

   我喜歡唱歌。

3. That's my favorite song.

   那是我最喜歡的歌曲。

 情境二：唱得如何？

4. You can sing really well.

   你唱得非常好。

5. Gosh, you're out of tune.

   噢，你唱走調了。

英文能力 UP！
Gosh 是表示驚訝的歎詞。

 情境三：聽聽音樂吧

6. Which CD do you want to listen to?

   你想聽哪張唱片？

7. I love this song.

   我喜歡這首歌。

8. I want to listen to it again.

   我想再聽一次。

9. I want to listen to it with headphones.

   我想用耳機來聽。

10.Can you play the song again?

   你能再播放那首歌嗎？

11.Can we play another CD?

   我們能播放其他唱片嗎？

Scene 46

做手工
Let's play with clay.
我們來玩黏土吧。

💬 Conversation 美國家庭這樣說

Boy: Mom, let's play with clay.

Mom: Okay. What are you going to make today?

Boy: I'm going to make a dragon today.

Mom: That sounds great. What color is your dragon going to be?

Boy: It's going to be green.

Mom: So let's use the green clay. Can you rub the clay for a while so it will mix well?

Boy: Alright.

英文能力 UP！

Alright 是 All right 的另一種寫法，意思是：好的、對了、沒問題，用來表示同意、許可、了解等，它的同義詞是 Okay。

Useful Expressions 活學活用

聆聽英文內容

 情境一：玩黏土

1. Which shape do you want to make?

   你想做什麼形狀？

2. I am going to make a rabbit / crocodile.

   我要做一隻白兔／一條鱷魚。

3. Press it firmly with your hands.

   用雙手緊緊按下去。

4. Put a lump between your palms and roll it.

   放一塊在手掌，然後搓揉它。

5. Opps! There's too much clay.

   啊！這裏太多黏土了。

 情境二：使用工具

6. Let's spread it with a roller.

   用滾筒把它壓開。

7. I will use the mold to make a heart / triangle / circle.

   我會用模子來做一個心形／三角形／圓形。

8. Let's use a knife.

   我們用刀吧。

9. Be careful when you are using the knife.

   你用刀的時候要小心。

 情境三：其他小手工

10. Let's do some paper folding.

    我們來摺紙吧。

11. Let's paint a picture.

    我們來畫圖畫吧。

Scene 47 跟寵物玩耍

Do dogs talk to each other?
小狗們會聊天嗎？

💬 Conversation 美國家庭這樣說

Boy: Mom, do dogs talk to each other?

Mom: Of course they talk to each other.

Boy: What do they talk about?

Mom: I don't know. Maybe they talk about other dogs. Maybe they talk about food, or about us!

Boy: What do they say about us?

Mom: Hmm, they may say, "It's getting late. Are you gonna take us for a walk?"

英文能力 UP！

Maybe 是副詞，用於不肯定的推測，意思是「也許、大概、可能」。例如：I'll finish my homework soon — maybe by 6.（我很快會完成功課──大概 6 點前就會完成。）

Useful Expressions 活學活用

 情境一：與寵物玩耍

1. Come on. Get the ball.

   來，抓住球。

2. Go get it!

   去，拿回來！

3. Don't bark!

   不要吠！

4. Let's take doggie for a walk.

   我們去遛遛狗吧。

> **英文能力 UP！**
> Doggie 或 doggy 屬於兒語，
> 特別用來指小狗或寵物。

 情境二：愛惜寵物

5. Don't pull the puppy's / kitten's tail.

   不要拉小狗 / 小貓的尾巴。

6. Can I fill doggie's water bowl?

   我可以在小狗的碗裏加點水嗎？

7. The birds / fish are hungry. May I give them a pinch of food?

   鳥兒 / 魚兒餓了，我可以給牠們餵點食物嗎？

 情境三：認識寵物

8. Birds have wings and lay eggs.

   鳥兒有翅膀，還會下蛋。

9. Fish have gills and live in the water.

   魚兒有鰓，住在水裏。

10. Frogs live both in water and on land.

    青蛙可以住在水裏或陸地。

11. Insects are animals, too. They have six legs. Some have wings.

    昆蟲也是動物。牠們有六條腿，有些還有翅膀。

Scene 48

栽種植物

Let's put some water in the vase.

我們在花瓶裏加點水吧。

💬 Conversation 美國家庭這樣説

Girl:　What plant is this, Mom?

Mom:　This is a lily. Smell it.

Girl:　It has a strong scent.

Mom:　Can you help take care of it?

Girl:　Sure. But how?

Mom:　Hmm, it seems like the flowers are thirsty.

Girl:　Let's put some water in the vase, shall we?

英文能力 UP！

It seems like 用來描述主觀的認知或感想，意思等於「看上去像」。例如：
It seems like it is real.（看上去像真的一樣。）

Useful Expressions 活學活用

聆聽英文內容

 ## 情境一：栽種植物的過程

1. Put the soil in the pot.

   把泥土放進盆子裏。

2. Let me put the seeds under the soil.

   我來把種子放在泥土下面。

3. Let me put the pot in a sunny spot.

   我來把盆子放在有陽光的地方。

4. The seeds will start to grow.

   種子會漸漸成長的。

 ## 情境二：給植物澆水

5. The soil is dry.

   泥土很乾。

6. I want to give it some water now.

   我現在想給它澆點水。

7. Let's water the flowers.

   我們來給花澆水吧。

8. Giving too much water might make the plant die.

   澆太多水的話，植物會死掉的。

9. How much water should I pour?

   我應該澆多少水呢？

 ## 情境三：認識植物

10. Trees and flowers are called plants.

    樹木和花朵都叫植物。

11. Plants have three parts: roots, stems, and leaves.

    植物有根、莖、葉三部分。

家長手記

家長讓孩子照料植物，不僅有助於培養他們的責任感（responsibility），還可以激發好奇心（curiosity）和想像力（imagination）呢！

109

Scene 49

游泳

I learnt to do free stroke today.
我今天學了自由式。

💬 **Conversation 美國家庭這樣說**

Mom: What did you learn in the swimming class today?

Girl: I learnt to do free stroke today. It's hard. I think breaststroke is more comfortable than free stroke.

Mom: What's the hardest part?

Girl: Kicking. Coach wants me to kick with a straight leg. It's hard because at the same time I need to reach my arm up in the air, plunge it into the water and pull the water toward myself.

Mom: I bet you can do it better if you work at it a little longer.

英文能力 UP！

游泳四式除了有 free stroke（自由式，又稱 freestyle）和 breaststroke（蛙式）之外，還有 backstroke（背泳）和 butterfly（蝶式）。

110

Useful Expressions 活學活用

聆聽英文內容

 情境一：游泳前的準備

1. Shower before you go in the pool.
   進游泳池前要先沖洗一下身體。

2. I'm going to change into my swimwear.
   我準備換上泳裝。

3. Don't forget your swim cap and goggles.
   不要忘記你的泳帽和蛙鏡。

4. Let's do some stretches.
   我們來做些伸展運動。

 情境二：游泳期間

> **英文能力 UP！**
>
>
> Swimwear 是泳裝的統稱，不分男女。女裝泳衣叫 swimsuit 或 bathing suit，兩件式泳衣叫 bikini。男裝的泳褲叫 swim shorts 或 swim trunks，三角泳褲叫 swim briefs 或 speedo。

5. Don't dive.
   不要跳水。

6. Don't splash water on others.
   不要讓水濺到其他人。

7. Mom will stick around in the pool area.
   媽媽會在游泳池附近。

8. The water is shallow / deep here.
   這裏的水很淺 / 深。

9. I have a cramp.
   我抽筋了。

 情境三：游泳完畢

10. I dry myself off with a towel.
    我用毛巾擦乾自己的身體。

11. Let's remove the air from your swim ring / floaty.
    我們把游泳圈 / 浮牀內的空氣擠出來吧。

Scene 50　球類活動

Can you get the ball to go into the basket?
你能把球投進籃球框嗎？

💬 Conversation 美國家庭這樣說

Mom: What was the best part of the school picnic today?

Boy: I played basketball with Colin and Irina. It was hard but I had fun playing with them.

Mom: Did you get the ball to go into the basket?

Boy: Yes, I did it twice. That made me feel really good. Colin played very well. He never missed a (shot).

投球

Mom: Awesome.

家長手記

在團體運動中，孩子通過和隊員交流，可以培養出團隊精神（teamwork）與體育精神（sportsmanship）。對孩子成長，還有今後的學業和事業都很有用。

Useful Expressions 活學活用

 情境一：投球

1. It's my turn to shoot the ball.
   輪到我投球了。

 情境二：傳球

2. I can throw the ball up high.
   我可以把球拋得很高。

3. Pass it to me.
   傳給我。

4. Catch the ball, Sweetie.
   把球接住，小甜心。

5. Here it goes! / Here we go!
   好，去吧！

6. Mom, throw it hard to me.
   媽，用力拋給我。

7. Oops, I missed it.
   啊，我沒接到。

8. Hit the ball with your hand.
   用手來打球。

9. Go and get the ball.
   去把球撿回來。

美國孩子的眾多課外
活動中，家長最重視
的是體育。孩子一般
在 4、5 歲甚至更早
就開始嘗試各種不同
的體育活動。

 情境三：踢球

10. I can kick the ball.
    我會踢球。

11. Can you kick it into the goal?
    你能把球踢進球門嗎？

113

Scene 51

跳舞
I'll dance in the talent show.
我會在才藝表演上跳舞。

💬 Conversation 美國家庭這樣說

Girl: Mom, I'm really looking forward to next week.

Mom: You've been excited all week! Is there anything you're looking forward to?

Girl: I can't wait to dance in the talent show.

Mom: What kind of dancing will you do this time?

Girl: Ballet. Mom, please come on time. 準時

Mom: I can't wait to see you on stage.

英文能力 UP！

「look forward to + 名詞 / 動名詞」的句型常在口語中使用，表達說話者急切期待的心情。例如：I'm really looking forward to the party / seeing you. （我十分期待派對那一天 / 與你見面。）

Useful Expressions 活學活用

聆聽英文內容

 情境一：興趣和志願

1. I go to dancing class once a week.

   我每星期上一次跳舞課。

2. My dream is to be a dancer / ballerina.

   我的夢想是要當上舞蹈員 / 芭蕾舞者。

 情境二：舞蹈的種類

3. I am learning ballet now.

   我正在學習芭蕾舞。

4. Do you like puppet dance / hip hop?

   你喜歡玩偶舞 / 街頭舞嗎？

5. I like fan dance / folk dance.

   我喜歡扇子舞 / 民族舞。

西方文化 GoGoGo!

Hip 是臀部，hop 指跳躍。街頭舞據說源自美國黑人社區，是一種節奏強烈的舞蹈形式。美國有舞蹈學校舉辦兒童街頭舞課程，特別為喜歡這種舞蹈的孩子而設。

 情境三：練習跳舞的過程

6. Let's do some stretching first.

   我們先做一下伸展運動。

7. It's hard to follow the moves.

   要跟上舞步很困難。

8. My legs hurt!

   我的腿很痛！

9. Just don't make fun of me if I trip and fall.

   如果我跌倒，不要取笑我。

10. Of course not! It's mostly for fun.

    當然不會！跳舞只是樂趣。

11. I'm sure you will do fine.

    我相信你一定會做到的。

Scene 52

樂器

I've always wanted to play the piano.
我一直想學彈鋼琴。

💬 Conversation 美國家庭這樣說

Mom: Here's a brochure for the after-school lessons. They're offering music classes.

Boy: That sounds interesting. What kind?

Mom: They teach almost every instrument there is!

Boy: Wow! I've always wanted to play the piano and the violin.

Mom: You can't do both at the same time. Just choose one.

西方文化 GoGoGo!

美國的《音樂心理學》（*Psychology of Music*）期刊指出，長期接受音樂訓練的兒童在閱讀方面，具有更好的認知能力（cognitive ability）。

Useful Expressions 活學活用

聆聽英文內容

 情境一：選擇喜歡的樂器

1. What instrument do you want to learn to play?
   你想學哪一種樂器？

2. I want to learn the violin.
   我想學小提琴。

3. I can play the piano.
   我會彈鋼琴。

4. I like to play the mouth organ.
   我喜歡吹口琴。

5. I want to learn to play the flute.
   我想學吹笛子。

> **英文能力 UP！**
> 表示樂器的名詞前一般要加上定冠詞 the，例如：to play the guitar（彈吉他）。

 情境二：上樂器班

6. I take piano lessons twice a week.
   我每星期上兩次鋼琴班。

7. I've been taking violin lessons since I was three.
   我從三歲開始就上小提琴班。

8. I have a flute class once a week.
   我每星期上一次笛子班。

情境三：學習樂器必須有恆心和毅力

9. My piano teacher is very strict.
   我的鋼琴老師很嚴厲。

10. Is it hard to memorize the whole piece?
    要記住整首曲子很難嗎？

11. Yes, it is. But I will try my best.
    是的，不過我會盡力而為。

繪畫

What are you drawing?
你在畫什麼呢？

💬 Conversation 美國家庭這樣說

Mom: What are you drawing, honey?

Boy: I'm drawing a lion.

Mom: Wow, what a cool picture of a lion! I like the bushy tail. You're choosing such great colors to draw your picture. Does this lion have a friend? Who is his friend?

Boy: A zebra. I'll draw a zebra.

Mom: Oh, will the lion eat the zebra?

Boy: No! They are friends.

Useful Expressions 活學活用

 情境一：一起來繪畫

1. Mom, I want to draw. Let's draw a picture.

   媽，我想繪畫。我們來畫圖畫吧。

2. What do you want to draw?

   你想畫什麼？

3. What do you want to draw with?

   你想用什麼來畫？

4. Color pencils / crayons / pastels.

   用顏色筆 / 蠟筆 / 粉彩來畫。

5. Color the picture.

   給圖畫塗上顏色吧。

 情境二：作品完成了

6. Look what I drew, Mom.

   媽，看我畫了什麼。

7. Wow, your drawing looks great!

   哇，你的圖畫看起來很棒！

8. Can you explain your drawing to me?

   你能解釋一下你的圖畫嗎？

9. Let's put your beautiful drawing on the wall.

   我們把你這幅美麗的圖畫掛在牆上吧。

10. Let me show Daddy my drawing.

    我去給爸爸看看我的圖畫。

 情境三：進一步引導

11. If you put more colors on it, the picture will look much better.

    如果你再多加一點顏色，你的圖畫看起來會更好。

119

Scene 54

珠心算

It's an abacus.

這是算盤。

💬 Conversation 美國家庭這樣説

Boy: Mom, what is this?

Mom: It's an abacus.

Boy: It looks so cute. It has so many little balls.

Mom: These little balls are the beads. An abacus has one hundred beads. They help you do simple math – like counting, addition, and subtraction.

Boy: So, what is 4 plus 5?

Mom: Do you want to try? It's fun and exciting.

Boy: Yes.

Useful Expressions 活學活用

聆聽英文內容

 情境一：運用算盤

1. Let's do some counting exercises with the abacus.

   我們用算盤來算算數吧。

 情境二：學習加法

2. Let's do a sum, like 4 + 3?

   來做一條加數，例如 4 加 3 是多少？

3. Let's move four beads, one by one, over to the left first.

   我們先把四顆珠逐一移到左邊。

4. Then, add three more.

   然後，再加三顆。

5. Push the beads together and count. How many beads do you see now?

   把這些珠都移在一起，算一下現在有多少顆？

6. Seven!

   七顆！

 情境三：學習減法

7. What's 9 minus 6?

   9 減 6 是多少？

8. Let's count and move nine beads first.

   我們先數九顆珠，把它們移過來。

9. Then, let's move back six beads.

   然後，把六顆珠移回去。

10. Count how many beads are left.

    算一下現在剩下多少顆珠。

11. Three!

    三顆！

西方文化 GoGoGo!

在美國，珠心算有等級考試。從 14 級起步，到 10 級可獲證書，6 級以上可獲獎盃，級數越小表示珠心算越厲害。

121

Scene 55

朗誦

I've joined the reciting competition.
我參加了朗誦比賽。

💬 Conversation 美國家庭這樣說

Mom: I can't hear you. When you recite a poem, you need to speak loudly enough for everyone in the class to hear you.

Girl: Okay. Let me try reading it aloud again.

Mom: Also, you need to face the audience. If you're looking at your shoes, your shoes can hear you really well, but other people might not.

Girl: I'm nervous, Mom.

Mom: Don't worry. If you keep on practicing, you will get better for sure.

英文能力 UP！

for sure 常用於口語，表示肯定，例如：No one knows for sure what really happened.（沒有人確切地知道發生了什麼事。）

Useful Expressions 活學活用

聆聽英文內容

 情境一：朗誦練習

1. Let me try reading out the poem loud.

   我來高聲地把詩歌唸出來吧。

2. Mom, can you record it and let me listen to it?

   媽，可以錄音給我聽嗎？

3. Read it slowly.

   慢慢地唸。

4. I want you to repeat after me as I read line by line.

   我一行一行唸，你跟着我唸吧。

5. Think about what the poem is about as you are reciting the lines.

   你朗讀這些詩句的時候，要想一想這首詩歌的內容是關於什麼。

 情境二：學好字詞的發音

6. I don't know how to read this word.

   我不知道這個單詞怎麼唸。

7. I can't really pronounce it.

   我發不出這個音。

8. You can always ask me.

   你隨時都可以問我。

9. What are the words that begin / end with the same sound?

   哪些單詞的開頭 / 結尾發同樣的音？

10. These two words rhyme with each other.

    這兩個單詞押韻。

英文能力 UP！

押韻（rhyming）是詩歌的特色之一。
它指在詩歌創作中，某些句子的結尾
使用韻母相同或相近的字，使朗讀句
子時有鏗鏘和諧的感覺。

Scene 56

話劇

What role are you playing?
你扮演什麼角色？

💬 Conversation 美國家庭這樣說

Boy: Mom, our class is going to do a play on Parents' Day.

Mom: That's great! What role are you playing?

Boy: I'm playing a prawn.

Mom: A prawn?! What is the play about? Is it a fairy tale?

Boy: Yes, it's a story about a mermaid! My teacher wants me
to play the prawn.

角色
Mom: What other characters are there?

Boy: There are many – a king, a queen, a prince, some crabs
and fish.

英文能力 UP！

Play 用作名詞時，其中一個意思是「戲劇」。用作動詞時，play 可以
指「扮演」某角色。

124

Useful Expressions 活學活用

聆聽英文內容

 ## 情境一：參與話劇演出

1. Mom, our class will do a play.
   媽，我班會做一齣話劇。

2. Do you have any role to play?
   你要扮演些什麼角色嗎？

3. I will play the emperor / princess / dwarf / witch.
   我會扮演國王 / 公主 / 小矮人 / 女巫。

 ## 情境二：角色扮演

4. Role play is fun.
   角色扮演很好玩。

5. I am a mermaid. I can swim.
   我是人魚，我會游泳。

6. I am a dragon. I can breathe fire.
   我是龍，我會噴火。

7. I am a fairy. I can fly.
   我是仙子，我會飛。

 ## 情境三：演出前那一晚

8. I'm so excited that I can't even sleep.
   我太興奮了，睡不着。

9. Mom, I'm nervous.
   媽，我好緊張。

10. Don't worry.
    不要擔心。

11. You can do it.
    你能做到的。

Scene 57

看電影

Let's go to the movies.

我們去看電影吧。

💬 Conversation 美國家庭這樣說

Mom:　Let's go to the movies. What do you want to see?

Girl:　What movies are showing today?

Mom:　Let's check it out. What about this one – *The Magic World?*

Girl:　That's a good choice. Is that a 3D movie? Do we need to get 3D glasses?

Mom:　Yes. Let's buy the tickets and get the glasses at the box office.

Girl:　Mom, can I get popcorn and a drink, too?

英文能力 UP！

The movies 相當於英式英語的 the cinema（電影院）。例如：We went to the movies / cinema last night.（昨晚我們去了看電影。）

Useful Expressions 活學活用

 情境一：去看電影

1. Let's see what movies are on.
   我們來看看有哪些電影在上映。

2. I want to watch a 3D movie / cartoon.
   我想看 3D 電影 / 動畫片。

3. Let me book the tickets online.
   我在網上訂票吧。

> **英文能力 UP！**
> 美式英語多用 movie，英式英語則多用 film。此外，picture 也可用來指電影。
>
>

 情境二：電影院裏

4. Wait in line here and then go in.
   在這裏排隊等待進去。

5. Mom, I want to go to the bathroom before the movie starts.
   媽，電影開始前，我想先去廁所。

6. Mom, it's dark inside. Can you find our seats?
   媽，裏面好暗。您能找到我們的座位嗎？

7. Watch your step.
   走路要小心。

8. I can't see because that tall man is blocking my view.
   我看不到，因為那個個子高的男人擋住了我。

9. Hush! Be quiet in the theater.
   噓！在電影院內要安靜。

> **英文能力 UP！**
> Hush! 是用來叫別人安靜下來的口語。
>
>

 情境三：談談對電影的感受

10. Did you like the movie?
    你喜歡這部電影嗎？

11. The movie was funny / boring / scary / exciting / cute.
    這部電影很有趣 / 沉悶 / 恐怖 / 刺激 / 可愛。

Scene 58　去超級市場

We're going to this supermarket.

我們去這間超級市場。

💬 Conversation 美國家庭這樣說

Boy:　Mom, are we going to the grocery store?

Mom:　No, the grocery store is closed. We're going to this supermarket. It stays open until nine thirty.

Boy:　Okay. Mom, can you get me ice cream?

Mom:　All right, but let's go to the household section first. I'm looking for detergent for the washing machine.

Boy:　Mom, I want to ride in the cart.

Mom:　Oh no, you're a big boy now. You are too heavy to ride in the cart.

家長手記

購物車（shopping cart）只允許 3 歲以下的兒童乘坐，超齡的孩子坐購物車容易導致翻車。在美國，每年有 24,000 個兒童因坐購物車而發生意外受傷。家長切記要小心！

Useful Expressions 活學活用

聆聽英文內容

 情境一：逛超級市場

1. Let's go to the supermarket to buy some goodies.

   我們去超級市場買些零食吧。

2. Let's go grocery shopping.

   我們去採購日常雜貨吧。

 英文能力 UP！

Goody 用於口語，指吸引人或合心意的東西，常用來表示好吃的食物。

 情境二：在超級市場裏

3. Go get a cart.

   去拉一台手推車過來。

4. Let's go to the fruit section first.

   我們先去蔬果區。

5. Give me 2 kilograms of it.

   給我 2 公斤。

6. Mom, ice creams are on sale.

   媽，冰淇淋減價了。

7. The cart is full.

   手推車滿了。

 **情境三：結賬**

8. Put the groceries on the counter.

   把這些食物雜貨放在櫃枱上。

9. Check if we forgot anything.

   確認一下我們有沒有忘記了什麼。

10. We've brought our own bag.

    我們有自備購物袋。

11. Let's put them in the bag.

    我們來把東西放進購物袋吧。

Scene 59

逛商場

Let's go shopping in the mall.
我們去商場購物吧。

💬 Conversation 美國家庭這樣說

Girl:　Mom, isn't this cute?

Mom:　It is.

Girl:　Can I have it?

Mom:　Didn't you just get a new toy last week?

Girl:　I want this one.

Mom:　Toys aren't on our list to buy today. And that's a big toy. That would be like a Christmas or birthday present. Do you want me to add it to your wish list? C'mon, let's go shopping in the mall.

> **英文能力 UP！**
> C'mon 是 come on 的縮寫，指「來吧」。

Useful Expressions 活學活用

 情境一：逛商場

1. Excuse me, where can I find children's magazines?

   請問一下，我可以在哪裏找到兒童雜誌呢？

2. Is there a toy shop in this mall?

   這個商場裏有玩具店嗎？

3. I am looking for toys / clothes / shoes.

   我在找玩具 / 衣服 / 鞋子。

4. I'm just looking.

   我只是隨便看看。

> **英文能力 UP！**
>
> Mall 是美式英語，全稱 shopping mall，英式英語的説法是 shopping centre。

 情境二：試穿衣服

5. Try this sweater / T-shirt / dress on.

   試穿這件毛衣 / T 恤衫 / 裙子。

6. The fitting room is over there.

   試身室就在那邊。

7. It fits you perfectly.

   這非常合身。

8. I (don't) like it.

   我很喜歡 / 不喜歡。

9. It's too small / big / wide / tight.

   這太小 / 大 / 鬆 / 緊了。

 情境三：找到合適的東西

10. I think this is what I want.

    這就是我想要的東西。

11. Could you wrap it up for me?

    可以給我包起來嗎？

Scene 60

坐巴士
When does the bus leave?
巴士是什麼時候離開的呢？

💬 Conversation 美國家庭這樣説

Girl:　Mom, when does the bus leave?

Mom:　It leaves every twenty minutes.

Girl:　Do you know when the next one is coming?

Mom:　Well, we actually just missed it.

Girl:　You mean we have to wait twenty whole minutes?!

Mom:　Unfortunately. Sometimes, though, it's a little faster.

Girl:　Too bad.

Mom:　We still have time. Be patient.

英文能力 UP！

Too bad. 常在口語中使用，通常是遇到不如意事時發出的感歎。例如：Too bad. I wonder if we'll still have enough time for shopping.（真倒霉，不知道我們還有沒有足夠時間去購物呢。）

Useful Expressions 活學活用

聆聽英文內容

 情境一：坐巴士

1. What number bus do we need to take?

   我們要坐幾號巴士？

2. The bus stop is over there.

   巴士站在那邊。

3. The bus is here. Let's get on.

   巴士來了，我們上車吧。

 情境二：支付車資

4. Where do I buy the bus ticket?

   我在哪裏買車票？

5. You buy it on the bus.

   你在巴士上買吧。

6. Put the coins in the fare box.

   把硬幣投入車資箱裏。

7. I have a tap card.

   我有拍卡。

8. Tap it on the ticket console.

   在售票機上拍一下。

情境三：坐巴士時要注意的事情

9. Keep your voice down.

   說話要輕聲點。

10. Don't put your head / hands out of the bus.

    不要把頭／手伸出車外。

11. Do not place your schoolbag on the seat next to you. Make space for others to sit.

    不要把書包放在你的座位旁邊，要給其他人讓出座位。

Scene 61

乘搭鐵路

Which platform should we go to?

我們要到哪個月台？

💬 Conversation 美國家庭這樣説

Boy:　Mom, which line do we need to take?

Mom:　We need to take the Island East line.

Boy:　Which platform should we go to?

Mom:　Platform number 3.

Boy:　It's right here. Look, the train is coming. Is that the train we need to take?

Mom:　Yes. Step behind the safety line. We'll get on the train after people get off.

西方文化 GoGoGo!

鐵路在不同地區有不同叫法，美國人叫 subway，英國人則叫 underground 或 tube。以「我們乘搭鐵路吧。」這句話為例，在外國分別可以説成：Let's take the subway / underground / tube / metro.

Useful Expressions 活學活用

聆聽英文內容

 情境一：乘搭鐵路

1. We are taking the subway today.

   我們今天乘搭鐵路。

2. How much more do we have to go?

   我們還要坐多久？

3. How many more stops are left?

   還有多少個站？

4. Five stops from here.

   還有五個站。

5. Do we get off at this station, or the next?

   我們要在這個站下車嗎？還是下一個？

 情境二：讓其他乘客進出

6. This is not our stop, Mom.

   媽，我們還沒到站。

7. We're not getting off. We just stand to the side of the door so that people may exit.

   我們不是要下車，只是站在車門旁邊讓其他人下車。

 情境三：其他乘搭鐵路的禮儀

8. Be careful, not to step on the foot of others.

   要小心點，不要踩到別人的腳。

9. Poles are for people to hold on to, for balance. So, do not lean on the poles.

   柱子是給人扶着，用來保持身體平衡，所以不要挨着柱子。

10. We don't eat or drink on the train because it is against the rules.

   我們不能在車廂裏吃喝，因為這是違反規則的。

Scene 62

遊樂場

Mom, I want to swing.

媽，我想盪鞦韆。

💬 Conversation 美國家庭這樣說

Girl:　Mom, I want to swing.

Mom:　Okay. Sit on the board and get comfortable. Do you want
　　　me to push you so you can swing very high?

　　　鞦韆板

Girl:　Yeah! Look at me. I'm flying this high!

Mom:　Wow, my sweetie is going up to the sky!

Girl:　Push me harder.

Mom:　Hold on tight! Don't fidget! It's going higher.

　　　抓緊

在美國，遊樂場裏的遊玩設施一般包括鞦韆（swing）、滑
梯（slide）、團團轉（roundabout）、蹺蹺板（seesaw /
teeter-totter）、攀爬架（climbing frame / monkey bars）、
沙土（sandpit / sandbox）、單槓（bar）等。

Useful Expressions 活學活用

聆聽英文內容

 情境一：盪鞦韆

1. Push me harder / slower.

   用力 / 輕輕地推我。

2. Mom, can you stop the swing? I want to get off.

   媽，可以幫我停住鞦韆嗎？我想下來了。

 情境二：溜滑梯

3. Climb up. Slide down now.

   爬上去，然後滑下來。

4. I can slide down by myself.

   我可以自己溜滑梯。

5. Mom, can you hold me?

   媽，您能扶住我嗎？

6. OK. Mom will catch you at the bottom.

   好的，媽媽會在（滑梯）底下接住你。

 情境三：要輪着玩

7. I've been waiting for quite a while.

   我等很久了。

8. I'm sure the other kids will finish up soon so that you can have your turn.

   我肯定其他小孩很快會玩完，馬上就輪到你了。

情境四：要注意安全！

9. It's dangerous to jump off the slide / swing.

   從滑梯 / 鞦韆上跳下來是很危險的。

10. I'll be careful when I pass around a moving swing.

    我經過擺動的鞦韆時會小心的。

Scene 63

去海邊
I want to build a sandcastle.
我想堆沙城堡。

💬 Conversation 美國家庭這樣說

Girl:　Mom, I'm done with swimming. Let's explore the tide pools. Maybe we'll find some crabs. Then we can put them in our aquarium!

Mom:　That's not a good idea, Sweetie. We're not going to hurt any living things.

Girl:　Okay. What are we going to do now?

Mom:　Let's collect some seashells, okay?

Girl:　I want to build a sandcastle instead. Mom, let's make one together. Let's also get some ice cream. Ice cream tastes great on the beach.

Useful Expressions 活學活用

聆聽英文內容

 情境一：去海邊玩

1. Let's go to the beach.
   我們去海灘吧。

2. There're a lot of people on the beach.
   海灘上有很多人。

 情境二：海邊的活動

3. I want to play Frisbee.
   我想玩飛碟。

4. Mom, let's build a sandcastle together.
   媽，我們一起來堆沙城堡吧。

5. Let's play ball.
   我們打球吧。

 情境三：要注意的事情

6. Swimming can be fun. Swimming can be dangerous, too.
   游泳可以很好玩，也可以很危險的。

7. Don't swim alone.
   不要一個人游泳。

英文能力 UP！

Suntan lotion 又稱 suntan oil。其他美式說法還包括：sunblock、sunscreen；英式的說法有 sun cream。

 情境四：不要給曬傷呀！

8. Let's put on some suntan lotion, Sweetie.
   小甜心，我們來塗些防曬油吧。

9. I think I got too much sun today.
   我覺得今天曬太陽曬過頭了。

10. Wow, you really got burnt!
    哇，你真的給曬傷了！

Scene 64

郊外遠足

We are finally at the top!
我們終於到達山頂了！

💬 Conversation 美國家庭這樣說

Boy:　We came all the way up here.

Mom:　Yay! We are finally at the top!

Boy:　That was a tough hike, Mom. My legs hurt.

Mom:　Come on, Sweetie. Walk up a little bit and look down over here.

Boy:　Wow, it's so beautiful! I can see the ocean from here! Hooray!

Mom:　It was hard at first, but it feels good here at the top, doesn't it?

Boy:　Yep!

> **英文能力 UP！**
> Yep! 是 yes 其中一個變體，其他說法還有 yea、yeah。

140

Useful Expressions 活學活用

 情境一：遠足前

1. Let's go hiking.

   我們去遠足吧。

2. I can't wait to go to the mountains.

   我等不及要爬到山上去。

3. What if it rains?

   如果下雨怎麼辦？

4. Don't worry. The weather will be nice, they say.

   別擔心，他們說天氣會很好。

 情境二：身處大自然的環境

5. The air feels so fresh and clean.

   這裏的空氣很清新潔淨呢。

6. The mountain looks so high!

   這座山看來很高呢！

 情境三：遠足的注意事項

7. Go up carefully.

   小心地走上去。

8. Follow the trail.

   沿着這條小徑走。

 情境四：感到累了

9. Let's rest for a little while / in the shade.

   我們休息一會吧 / 我們在陰涼的地方休息吧。

10. Want to drink some water?

    要喝點水嗎？

Scene 65

出發了

That will be a wonderful vacation!

那將會是美好的假期！

💬 Conversation 美國家庭這樣說

Boy:　Mom, what are we going to do for summer vacation?　以及

Mom:　This year we're going to New York, and California as well.

Boy:　California? Where is it?

Mom:　It's in America.

Boy:　What places are we going to see?

Mom:　Most of the major cities in California, such as San Francisco and Los Angeles. That will be a wonderful vacation.

Boy:　Yay! I can't wait for the vacation!

英文能力 UP！

Vacation 指「假期」，多用於美式英語，英式英語則多用 holidays 來表示。

142

Useful Expressions 活學活用

聆聽英文內容

 情境一：計劃去旅遊

1. Let's plan a vacation. Where do you want to go?

   我們來計劃一下旅行吧，你想去什麼地方？

2. Are we going on a package tour?

   我們是參加旅行團的嗎？

3. We're traveling on our own this time.

   這次我們自己去。

 情境二：選擇目的地

4. I want to go somewhere warm.

   我想去一個天氣和暖的地方。

5. I want to spend time on beaches.

   我想去海邊度假。

6. We could visit Thailand / Korea / Canada.

   我們可以去泰國 / 韓國 / 加拿大。

 情境三：出發前的準備

7. Let's pack our bags.

   我們來收拾行李吧。

8. Don't forget my passport.

   不要忘記帶我的護照。

 情境四：出發去機場

9. Mom, what's the best way of getting to the airport?

   媽，我們怎樣去機場是最好的呢？

10. Well, we can take the airport bus / subway.

    嗯，我們可以坐機場巴士 / 鐵路。

Scene

66

在機場

Can I have your passports, please?
請把你們的護照給我，好嗎？

Conversation 美國家庭這樣說

Staff:　Can I have your passports, please?

Mom:　Here you are.

Staff:　Will you put the baggage on the scale, please?

Boy:　Mom, let me put the bags on the scale.

Mom:　No. They're too heavy for you. Can you look after the hand luggage? I'll cope with these cases on the trolley.

Boy:　All right.　　　　處理

英文能力 UP！

Baggage 和 luggage 均指「行李」：美國多用 baggage，英國則多用 luggage。兩個單詞都是不可數名詞，如要說「一件行李」，可用 a piece 或 an item，例如：We have three pieces of baggage / luggage.（我們有三件行李。）

144

Useful Expressions 活學活用

聆聽英文內容

 情境一：辦理登機手續

1. Let's check our bags at the check-in desk.
   我們去登記櫃枱托運行李吧。

2. We need to check in two hours before the flight.
   我們需要在起飛兩個小時前辦理登機手續。

3. I'll take this small bag with me.
   我會隨身帶着這個小包。

4. Here is your boarding pass.
   這是你的登機證。

 情境二：通過海關

5. Put your jacket and bag through the X-ray machine.
   把你的外套和袋子放在輸送帶上通過 X 光機檢查。

6. When I walk through the metal detector, will it beep?
   我通過金屬探測機時，它會發出「嗶嗶」的響聲嗎？

 情境三：準備登機

7. Mom, our flight leaves from Gate 10.
   媽，我們的航班從 10 號閘口出發。

8. It'll begin boarding at 10:15.
   10 點 15 分開始登機。

9. What is our flight number?
   我們的航班編號是什麼？

10. Is the flight on time?
    航班準時嗎？

11. There's a 20-minute delay.
    會有 20 分鐘的延誤。

英文能力 UP！

Flight 一般分為 international flight（國際航班）和 domestic flight（國內航班）。長途航班叫 a long-haul flight，而轉接航班則叫 a connecting flight。

Scene 67　在飛機上

Let's fasten our seatbelts.
我們來把安全帶扣好吧。

💬 Conversation 美國家庭這樣說

Boy:　Mom, I like a window seat!

Mom:　Why are you so excited about sitting there?

Boy:　I like being able to look outside. I just like looking out at the sky.

Mom:　You have nothing to see but clouds. They're all the same.

Boy:　No, they are not! They're changing all the time. There might be aliens or UFOs, too.

Mom:　Oh really? So let's fasten our seatbelts first, then we'll be safe.

Boy:　Okay.

Useful Expressions 活學活用

聆聽英文內容

 情境一：飛機起飛前

1. My seat number is 18B.

   我的座位編號是 18B。

2. Let's put our bags in the overhead bins.

   我們來把袋子放在艙頂行李箱裏。

3. May I have the window seat?

   我可以坐靠窗的座位嗎？

4. Mom, the plane is taking off!

   媽，飛機起飛了！

除了 window seat 外，飛機上還有以下座位：aisle seat，即靠近走道的座位；bulkhead seat（隔間座），這位置前沒有乘客，而是飛機隔間牆；exit row seat（逃生門座），這座位的空間比較大。

 情境二：跟機艙服務員說說話

5. May I have a pillow?

   可以給我一個枕頭嗎？

6. May I have a blanket?

   可以給我一張毛毯嗎？

7. May I have some water?

   可以給我水嗎？

 情境三：準備降落了

8. We're coming in to land.

   我們快要着陸了。

9. Is your seatbelt on?

   你扣好了安全帶沒有？

10. I'm putting my seatbelt on now.

   我現在扣上安全帶。

11. We cannot leave our seats until the plane has stopped.

   飛機還沒有停好，我們都不能離開座位。

Scene 68 入住酒店
Where's our hotel, Mom?
媽，酒店在哪裏？

💬 Conversation 美國家庭這樣説

Boy: I'm so tired!

Mom: Me, too! That's the longest flight I've ever ridden.

Boy: Where's our hotel, Mom?

Mom: I have the address right here. It's not too far.

Boy: The first thing I want to do when checking into the hotel room is to take a spa bath.

Mom: Good! I've booked a room with a fantastic view of the sea. You'll love it.

英文能力 UP！

View 指「視野、景色」，例如：From the rooftop you get a panoramic view of the city.（從天台你可看到城市的全景。）

Useful Expressions 活學活用

聆聽英文內容

 情境一：住進酒店

1. Here is our room key.
   這是我們房間的鑰匙。

2. Mom, what is our room number?
   媽，我們住幾號房間？

3. Wow, the view looks so beautiful!
   哇，這裏的景色真美！

4. The view is fantastic! We can see the whole city!
   景色真美，整個城市一覽無遺！

 情境二：酒店的設施

5. Does this hotel have a swimming pool?
   這酒店有游泳池嗎？

6. Yes, there is one on the rooftop.
   有，頂樓就有一個。

7. I want to go there as soon as I can.
   我馬上就想到那裏去。

 情境三：酒店的服務

8. Mom, when is breakfast served?
   媽，早餐是什麼時候供應的呢？

9. Do we need any room service?
   我們需要送餐服務嗎？

10. We'll have a wake-up call at 7 in the morning.
    明天早上 7 點會有人把我們叫醒。

11. We need to check out by 12.
    我們必須在 12 點之前退房。

Scene 69

觀光

The scenery there is very beautiful.

那裏的風景很漂亮。

💬 Conversation 美國家庭這樣説

Boy:　Mom, what places are we going to see?

Mom:　Today we're going to Mount Shasta.

Boy:　Mount Shasta?

Mom:　It is one of the highest mountains in California. And it's a volcano.

Boy:　Is it beautiful? How far is it?

Mom:　Yes, the scenery there is very beautiful. It's quite far away so we need to hurry.

英文能力 UP！

Scenery 是不可數名詞，人們會説 What beautiful scenery!（多漂亮的風景！），而不説 What a beautiful scenery!

Useful Expressions 活學活用

聆聽英文內容

 情境一：參觀旅遊景點

1. What places are we going to visit today?
   我們今天會去什麼地方呢？

2. We're going to visit a theme park / zoo / cathedral today.
   我們今天去遊覽主題公園 / 動物園 / 大教堂。

3. We're going to see a waterfall / lake / volcano.
   我們去看瀑布 / 湖泊 / 火山。

4. We're going to the national park / mountains / seashore.
   我們會去國家公園 / 登山 / 海邊。

 情境二：參觀博物館

5. What time does the museum close today?
   今天博物館什麼時候關門呢？

6. Are there any special exhibitions on right now?
   現在有些什麼特別的展覽嗎？

 情境三：認識當地的文化

7. What language do people speak here?
   這裏的人說什麼語言的呢？

8. Where can we try the local food / street eats?
   我們可以在哪裏吃到當地的食物 / 街頭小吃？

 情境四：稱讚漂亮的風景

9. That's a stunning view!
   多麼漂亮的風景！

10. This is the most beautiful place I've ever been to!
    我從來沒有去過這麼漂亮的地方！

Scene 70

問路
Which way is Water World?
水世界在哪裏呢？

💬 Conversation 美國家庭這樣説

Boy:　Mom, which way is Water World?

Mom:　I don't know. Let's ask someone.

Boy:　How about that lady sitting on the bench?

Mom:　Okay.

Boy:　Hi! May we ask you a question?

Lady:　Sure. What is it?

Mom:　Could you tell us how to get to Water World?

英文能力 UP！

Could you tell us how to get to...?（請問……是往哪邊走？）是常見的問路句式。在句式前加上 Excuse me，會顯得客氣一點；隨意一點則可以説：How do I get to...?

Useful Expressions 活學活用

 ## 情境一:帶着地圖去旅行

1. Excuse me, how do I get to Central Park?
   請問中央公園在哪兒?

2. Could you show me on the map?
   你可以在這地圖上指示出來嗎?

3. We should keep walking until we come to a fountain, then turn right.
   我們應一直走,看見一座噴泉的時候向右拐。

4. How far do I walk?
   要走多遠?

 ## 情境二:查問地址或交通情況

5. This is the park / museum / restaurant I am looking for.
   我在找這個公園 / 博物館 / 餐廳。

6. Where is the nearest train station?
   最近的火車站在哪裏?

7. Excuse me, which bus goes to the national park?
   請問哪一輛巴士去國家公園的呢?

 ## 情境三:想確定方向

8. Is this the way to Ocean World?
   這是往海洋世界的路嗎?

9. You bet.
   一點都沒錯。

 ## 情境四:感謝途人協助

10. Thanks a lot for your help.
    非常感謝你的幫忙。

153

Scene 71

拍照片

Let's take a picture.
我們拍照吧。

💬 Conversation 美國家庭這樣說

Boy: Let's take a picture here, Mom.

Mom: Okay. Will you pose for my camera? Right. Now, move back a bit. Okay. One, two, three. Say cheese!

Boy: Cheese!

Mom: OK. One more. This time let's make a funny face. Great!

Boy: Mom, show me the picture. Oh, it doesn't look good.

Mom: The camera was shaking. Let's take another one.

西方文化 GoGoGo!

美國人在提出要拍照時，一般會說 Let's take a picture. 或簡單一句 Pictures time! / Photo time! 而準備拍照時會說 Say cheese，也有的人會說 Say C。因為 C 和 cheese 一樣，都能夠讓你露出美麗的牙齒。

Useful Expressions 活學活用

聆聽英文內容

 情境一：拍照時的位置與姿勢

1. Step ahead a little. / Move back a bit.
   往前站一點。 / 往後退一點。

2. Move to the right / left.
   往左邊 / 右邊移一點。

3. Everyone, squeeze together.
   各位，靠在一起。

 情境二：記住要微笑呀！

4. You look nervous. Try to look good.
   你看起來很緊張，擺出帥氣的樣子吧。

5. Smile for the camera.
   對着鏡頭微笑。

6. Make a big smile, please.
   請給我一個大大的微笑。

 情境三：找途人幫忙拍照

7. Let's ask someone to take a picture of us.
   我們去請其他人幫我們拍照吧。

8. Excuse me, could you take a picture of us?
   請問你可以幫我們拍照嗎？

情境四：來看看照片

9. Wow, it looks great!
   哇，這張看起來很好！

10. You look great in the picture.
    你很上鏡。

Scene 72

買紀念品

How much are these postcards?
這些明信片多少錢？

Conversation 美國家庭這樣說

Boy: Let's stop and look at the souvenirs at the souvenir stand.

Mom: What types of souvenirs are you looking for?

Boy: I want to buy something that you can't get anywhere else.

Mom: They've got mugs and fridge magnets. They've got postcards, too.

Boy: How much are these postcards?

Mom: They're 3 for 5 dollars.

Boy: I only need two.

Mom: If you buy them individually, they're 2 dollars each.

Useful Expressions 活學活用

聆聽英文內容

 情境一：賣紀念品的地方

1. There's a store down the street that sells souvenirs.

   這條街的盡頭有一間紀念品店。

2. Let's go there.

   我們去那裏看看吧。

3. Do you sell any souvenirs here?

   這裏有紀念品賣嗎？

 情境二：想買紀念品

4. Is there anything in particular you're looking for?

   你有些什麼特別想要買的嗎？

5. I want to buy some souvenirs for my friends.

   我想給朋友買些紀念品。

6. I want to buy a local gift for Grandma.

   我想給祖母買一份當地的禮物。

7. I'm looking for some unique local crafts.

   我在找一些獨特的當地手工藝品。

西方文化 GoGoGo!

Souvenir 本來是法語，後來引入英語中使用。作為英語，它只解作紀念品，但在法語中還有 memory（回憶）的意思呢。

 情境三：選購紀念品

8. These plates with names of cities are beautiful.

   這些印有城市名稱的碟子很漂亮。

9. These tourist T-shirts / caps look nice.

   這些遊客 T 恤衫 / 帽子看來很不錯。

10. I'd rather buy these homemade chocolates / scented soaps / signature cookies.

    我寧願買這些自製巧克力 / 香皂 / 特色甜餅乾。

Scene 73

生日

My birthday is coming up.

我的生日快到了。

💬 Conversation 美國家庭這樣說

Girl: Mom, I'm happy that my birthday is coming up.

Mom: Do you want to invite your classmates over for a party?

Girl: Yeah! I want to invite all of my classmates.

Mom: **I'm afraid** we don't have enough room for all your classmates. You may want to invite some of your very best friends only.

Girl: But I want to invite all of them. They are all my best friends.

Mom: Okay, let's book a restaurant for your party this year.

英文能力 UP！

I'm afraid 用於口語，表示抱歉、惋惜或委婉拒絕，例如：I can't help you, I'm afraid.（我幫不了你，對不起。）

Useful Expressions 活學活用

聆聽英文內容

 情境一：生日快到了

1. I can't wait for my birthday.
   我很想生日快些來到。

 情境二：我的生日禮物

2. What present do you want for your birthday?
   你想收到什麼生日禮物？

3. I want a doll / model car for my birthday.
   我想要洋娃娃／模型車作為生日禮物。

4. I got a birthday card from my friend.
   我收到朋友給我的生日卡。

5. Wow! I really like this present.
   哇！我真的很喜歡這份禮物。

 情境三：生日的意義

6. What's the best birthday present you've ever received, Mom?
   媽，您收到過最好的生日禮物是什麼？

7. To me, a birthday is a day to bring people together. It's a day to celebrate all the love that surrounds you.
   對我來說，生日是把人們聚集起來的一天。在這一天，我知道身邊有多少愛，這是我要慶祝的事情。

 情境四：感謝前來參加派對的朋友

8. Thanks for coming to my party.
   謝謝你來參加我的派對。

9. Thank you everyone for the birthday wishes. I love you all.
   謝謝你們每一位的生日祝福，我愛你們。

Scene 74

參加生日會

When is the birthday party?

生日會在什麼時候舉行？

💬 Conversation 美國家庭這樣說

Boy: Mom, Colin invited me to his birthday party.

Mom: Oh, that sounds good. When is the birthday party?

Boy: This coming Sunday. What should I give him for a present?

Mom: Well, think of something that he likes.

Boy: Hmm, Colin likes to read. Can I get him a comic book?

Mom: Why not?

英文能力 UP！

Why not? 用來表示同意，當對方提出一項建議，你可以用 Why not? 來表示贊成。如有人說 Let's get her a Barbie doll.（我們給她送一個芭比娃娃吧。）就可回答 Why not?（好啊。）

Useful Expressions 活學活用

聆聽英文內容

 情境一：獲邀參加生日會

1. I got an invitation from my classmate.
   我從同學那裏收到了邀請函。

2. Where is she / he going to have the party?
   他 / 她要在哪裏開派對？

 情境二：準備禮物

3. Let's buy a present for him / her.
   我們給他 / 她買一份禮物吧。

4. I'm going to write a birthday card.
   我要寫生日卡。

 情境三：來切蛋糕！

5. Let's sing *Happy Birthday*.
   我們來唱生日歌。

6. Make a wish first.
   先許個願吧。

7. Blow out the candles.
   把蠟燭吹滅。

西方文化 GoGoGo!

生日吹蠟燭和許願的習俗源於希臘。古希臘人崇敬月亮女神，會在聖壇上擺上插着蠟燭的糕點。後來這習俗傳入民間，人們相信燃燒的蠟燭具有神奇的力量，如果孩子能一口氣吹滅所有蠟燭，他便可如願以償。

 情境四：送上禮物與祝福

8. Happy birthday! / Have a good time!
   祝你生日快樂！/ 玩開心點！

9. Here's my present.
   這是我送給你的禮物。

10. Open your gift, please.
    請打開禮物。

Scene 75

父親節和母親節

Daddy knows that you love him.
爸爸知道你愛他的。

💬 Conversation 美國家庭這樣説

Girl: Mom, I don't know what to give Daddy for Father's Day.

Mom: Why don't you give him a card?

Girl: I already wrote a card, but I want to give him a present, too.

Mom: A card is enough.

Girl: No, I have to find a gift for Daddy. Daddy takes care of me 〔照顧〕 and I love him so much.

Mom: You're such a good girl. Daddy knows that you love him.

多德夫人（Dodd）的母親很早死去，父親一直父兼母職，把 6 個兒女培育成人。她的父親死後，多德夫人開始推動成立父親節的運動。美國過去只有母親節，到 1924 年，政府終於宣布父親節成為美國的節日。

Useful Expressions 活學活用

 情境一：父親節和母親節

1. Mother's / Father's Day is next week.
   下星期就是母親節 / 父親節了。

2. Sunday is Mother's / Father's Day.
   星期日就是母親節 / 父親節了。

 情境二：送上心意與祝福

3. Mom / Dad, this is my present for you.
   媽 / 爸，這是我送給您的禮物。

4. The gift is something that I drew.
   這份禮物是我畫的圖畫。

5. This is a paper carnation I made at school.
   這是我在學校用紙做的一朵康乃馨。

6. Let me sing a song for you.
   我給您唱首歌吧。

7. Mom / Dad, do you like this gift?
   媽 / 爸，您喜歡這份禮物嗎？

8. Thank you, Sweetie. I like this very much.
   謝謝你，小甜心。我非常喜歡。

康乃馨（carnation）被稱為母親之花。母親節的時候，美國人會用康乃馨來表達對母親的感恩和思念之情。

情境三：我最愛的爸爸媽媽

9. I love you, Mom / Dad.
   媽 / 爸，我愛您。

10. You're the best Mom / Dad in the world.
    您是世界上最好的媽媽 / 爸爸。

11. I'll be a better son / daughter from now on.
    從現在開始，我會當一個更好的兒子 / 女兒。

163

Scene 76

地球日

We must save the Earth.

我們必須保護地球。

💬 Conversation 美國家庭這樣說

Mom: Do you know what today is?

Girl: Yes, it's April 22.

Mom: It's more than just a date. It's Earth Day.

Girl: What's that, Mom?

Mom: It's a yearly reminder to take care of our planet.

Girl: Oh, you mean like reuse things and recycle stuff?

Mom: Yes. We must save the Earth, save water, and stop using plastic bags.

西方文化 GoGoGo!

世界地球日的主題是 Only One Earth（只有一個地球）。面對日益惡化的地球生態環境，成人和孩子都有責任和義務行動起來，保護我們的家園。

Useful Expressions 活學活用

聆聽英文內容

 情境一：地球生病了

1. The Earth is sick now.
   地球現在生病了。

2. The smoke from cars is polluting the air.
   汽車排放的黑煙污染了空氣。

3. Industrial waste is polluting the water.
   工業廢料污染了海水。

 情境二：保護地球的方法

4. How can we protect our Earth?
   我們可以怎樣保護地球呢？

5. We need to think green.
   我們必須有環保思維。

6. What can we do to save water?
   我們怎樣做可以節省水資源？

7. We should save water by trying to use less.
   我們應該試着減少用水來節省水資源。

8. How about if I take shorter showers?
   我把淋浴的時間縮短可以嗎？

9. That's a good idea, because showers waste a lot of water.
   這個主意不錯，因為淋浴用很多水。

 情境三：循環再造的意思

10. Mom, what's recycling?
    媽，什麼是循環再造？

11. It's when we try to use old things again.
    循環再造是我們試着把舊的東西重新使用。

Scene 77　感恩節

Why do we eat turkey on Thanksgiving?
為什麼我們會在感恩節吃火雞？

💬 Conversation 美國家庭這樣說

Boy: Mom, how did you celebrate Thanksgiving when you were my age?

Mom: It's no different from what we're doing today. We spend time with family and friends. We sit down together for Thanksgiving dinner. We talk, we pray, and then we eat.

Boy: Why do we eat turkey on Thanksgiving?

Mom: According to legend, people hunted for turkey for food on the very first Thanksgiving Day. It has then become a custom for our country.

西方文化 GoGoGo!

火雞（turkey）是很多美國家庭在感恩節那天必吃的食物，所以 Thanksgiving Day 又叫 Turkey Day。

Useful Expressions 活學活用

聆聽英文內容

 情境一：感恩節的意義

1. Mom, why do people celebrate Thanksgiving?
   媽，為什麼人們要慶祝感恩節？
2. That's a day of giving thanks for all that we have.
   在這一天，我們對自己擁有的所有東西表示感恩。
3. Let's say a prayer before eating.
   我們吃飯前先來禱告吧。

 情境二：想一想要感恩的人或事

4. Who is someone you could say "thank you" to today?
   And why?
   誰是今天你要跟他說「謝謝」的人呢？為什麼？
5. Think about what you're thankful for, including even the smallest things.
   就算是很小的事情也好，想一想你有什麼值得感恩。
6. Spending time with Mom and Dad makes me happy.
   和爸爸媽媽在一起，讓我感到快樂。
7. How does it make you feel when you do something really nice for someone else?
   你為別人做了一件好事，會有什麼感覺？
8. It makes me feel great.
   我會覺得很開心。

情境三：感恩節的活動

9. Let's go to Mass on Thanksgiving Day.
   我們去參加感恩彌撒吧。

Scene 78 萬聖節
Trick or treat!
不給糖果就搗蛋！

💬 Conversation 美國家庭這樣說

Boy: Is anyone home?

Neighbor: Yes. What do you want, Mr. Vampire?

Boy: Trick or treat!

Neighbor: Oh come on, I don't have any candies for you.

Boy: You can give me some pennies then. 　美加地區的
一分硬幣

Neighbor: Unfortunately I don't have any pennies either.

Boy: If you don't treat me, I will trick you!

Neighbor: Wow, I'm so scared! Okay, I will give you some candies.

以下這些是最受美國孩子歡迎的萬聖節服裝：ghost（鬼）、
vampire（吸血僵屍）、witch（女巫）、zombie（喪屍）、
werewolf（人狼）。你會選擇哪一種呢？

Useful Expressions 活學活用

聆聽英文內容

 情境一：迎接萬聖節

1. Mom, we're going to have a Halloween party at school.

   媽，學校將會舉辦萬聖節派對。

2. What costume are you going to wear to the party?

   你準備穿什麼化妝服裝去參加派對呢？

3. There are lots of different scary monsters to choose from.

   有不少恐怖的怪獸給你選擇。

4. I think I'll go as a vampire.

   我打算扮吸血僵屍。

5. Let's dress up as a monster.

   我穿成怪獸的樣子吧。

6. That's a good choice.

   真是不錯的選擇呀。

 情境二：布置家居

7. Let's decorate our house and try to make it look scary.

   我們把家裝飾一下，讓家裏看來恐怖些。

8. Let's carve a scary face into the pumpkin.

   我們在南瓜上雕個鬼臉吧。

9. All the decorations with cobwebs are very nice.

   這些蜘蛛網的裝飾品很不錯呀。

 情境三：慶祝萬聖節

10. Let's watch a scary movie.

    我們來看恐怖電影吧。

11. I'll go trick-or-treating and get lots of candies.

    我去玩「不給糖果就搗蛋」，會拿到很多糖果的。

Scene 79

聖誕節

I'll decorate the Christmas tree.
我會布置聖誕樹。

💬 Conversation 美國家庭這樣説

Girl: Christmas is just a few days away. I really like this time of the year.

Mom: Yes, I like it too. You know, Grandpa and Grandma are coming for Christmas.

Girl: Wow! That's great news.

Mom: Can you help me put up the Christmas tree?

Girl: Sure. I'll decorate the Christmas tree. After that I'll put my stocking under the Christmas tree so Santa will put my present in it.

英文能力 UP！

Santa 是聖誕老人（Santa Claus）的簡稱。在英國，人們會稱聖誕老人作 Father Christmas。

Useful Expressions 活學活用

 情境一：迎接聖誕節

1. I love Christmas the most.

   我最喜歡的就是聖誕節。

2. Let's decorate the Christmas tree.

   我們來布置聖誕樹吧。

3. I can't wait to see it when it's done.

   我想儘快看到聖誕樹裝飾完成的模樣。

4. I am going to make some Christmas cards for my friends.

   我會做一些聖誕卡送給朋友。

 情境二：互相祝福

5. Merry Christmas!

   聖誕快樂！

6. May your life be filled with love, peace, and joy!

   願你的生命充滿愛、和平和快樂！

 情境三：聖誕節的活動

7. Let's throw a Christmas party.

   我們來舉辦聖誕派對吧。

8. Let's sing a Christmas carol.

   我們來唱聖誕頌吧。

9. Let's make a snowman together.

   我們一起來做個雪人吧。

10. I can't wait for the big Christmas dinner.

   我非常期待那頓聖誕大餐。

 家長手記 聖誕節時，家長可帶領孩子用英語唱Christmas Carols，例如：*Silent Night*（《平安夜》）、*Joy to the World*（《普世歡騰》）、*White Christmas*（《白色聖誕》）、*Jingle Bells*（《聖誕鐘聲》）等。

Scene 80

新年

Happy New Year!

新年快樂！

💬 Conversation 美國家庭這樣說

Girl: Happy New Year, Mom!

Mom: Happy New Year, Sweetie! What's your New Year's resolution?

Girl: Resolution?

Mom: I mean, what are your hopes for the New Year?

Girl: My greatest hope is to go to Disneyland. What about you, Mom?

Mom: My greatest hope is that I can laugh as much as I can.

Girl: That's so cool, Mom.

Useful Expressions 活學活用

聆聽英文內容

 情境一：新年的祝福

1. Have a Happy New Year!
   新年快樂！

2. I wish you good luck this year!
   祝你今年時來運到！

 情境二：新年的計劃

3. Do we have any plans for the New Year?
   我們新年有什麼計劃嗎？

4. We will have a New Year party.
   我們會開新年派對。

5. Are we going to see the fireworks?
   我們會去看煙火嗎？

6. Mom, do we get to celebrate two New Year Days this year again?
   媽，我們今年同樣要過兩次新年嗎？

7. Yes. We will go back to Hong Kong to celebrate the Chinese New Year with Grandma and Grandpa, but that is not until February.
   對，我們會回去香港跟祖母和祖父一起過農曆新年，但那將會是二月的事情。

 情境三：許下願望，憧憬將來

8. Let's make a New Year's wish, Mom.
   媽，我們來許新年願望吧。

9. What do you think will happen to you next year?
   你認為在新一年裏，會有什麼事情發生在你身上呢？

Scene 81

打招呼

Can you say hello to him, please?
可以請你跟他打招呼嗎？

💬 Conversation 美國家庭這樣說

Mom: Sweetie, do you remember Uncle Pang? Can you say hello to him, please?

Boy: Hello, Uncle Pang!

Uncle: Hello, George! How are you doing?

Mom: George, when people ask you how you are, tell them and then ask them how they are.

Boy: How are you, Uncle Pang?

Uncle: I'm good. Thank you. I'm glad you came to see me.

英文能力 UP！

How are you (doing)? 就是「你好嗎？」的意思，人家問你 How are you? 的時候，你可以這樣回答：I'm good. Thank you. And you?（很好，謝謝，你呢？）

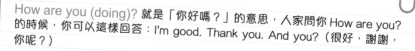

174

Useful Expressions 活學活用

聆聽英文內容

 情境一：見面時打招呼

1. Hello, how are you?
   哈囉，你好嗎？

2. Good to see you!
   很高興見到你！

3. I haven't seen you for a long time. How have you been?
   很久沒見了，你近來好嗎？

4. It's been (a while) 一段頗長的時間
   好久不見了。

5. How's everything going?
   一切順利嗎？

 情境二：打招呼的禮儀

6. Greet your teacher with a smile every morning.
   每天早上微笑着向老師打招呼。

7. Look people you meet in the eye, smile and say "hello".
   打招呼時要看着對方的眼睛，微笑，然後説「哈囉」。

 情境三：道別時也要打招呼啊！

8. Goodbye!
   再見！

9. See you again.
   下次見。

10. Bye. See you then.
    再見，到時見。

11. See you on Monday.
    星期一見。

西方文化 GoGoGo!

在美國，孩子和其他人説話時，家長有時會在旁邊提醒：「説話時要看着人家的眼睛呀。」

Scene 82

認識新朋友

Nice to meet you.
很高興認識你。

💬 Conversation 美國家庭這樣說

Boy:　May I sit here?

Girl:　Sure. Are you a student here?

Boy:　Yes, I am. My name's George. What's yours?

Girl:　My name's Irina. Nice to meet you.

Boy:　Nice to meet you, too. How do you spell your name?

Girl:　It's I.R.I.N.A. Irina.

英文能力 UP！

Nice to meet you 和 Nice meeting you 都是初次跟人家見面時用的客套語，意思是「很高興認識你」。跟初次相見者道別時，要再一次表示 It was nice to meet you 或 It was nice meeting you.（很高興認識了你。）

176

Useful Expressions 活學活用

 情境一：跟新朋友打招呼

1. Nice to meet you, Irina.

   艾雲娜，很高興認識你。

2. I'm glad to meet you. Please call me George.

   很高興認識你，你可以叫我佐治。

3. I'm happy to have met you.

   我很高興認識你。

4. How do you do?

   你好嗎？

5. I've heard a lot about you.

   我聽説了很多關於你的事。

6. Let's shake hands.

   我們來握手吧。

英文能力 UP！

人家問你 How do you do? 的時候，你只要同樣回答 How do you do? 就可以了。

 情境二：給媽媽介紹新朋友

7. Mom, I'd like you to meet my friend, Irina. She's from Canada.

   媽，我想給您介紹我的新朋友——艾雲娜。她是加拿大人。

8. These are my parents.

   他們是我的父母。

 情境三：認識新朋友

9. Where do you go to school?

   你在哪裏上學？

10. When is your birthday?

    你什麼時候生日？

11. How many brothers and sisters do you have?

    你有多少個兄弟姐妹？

Scene 83 自我介紹
I'm six years old.
我六歲。

💬 Conversation 美國家庭這樣說

Teacher: George, can you introduce yourself to your classmates?

Boy: Hello, everybody. My name's George. I'm six years old. There are four people in my family. My mom, dad, my younger sister Anna, and me. We have a dog and his name is Roger.

Teacher: What are some of your hobbies, George?

Boy: My favorite hobby is playing with Roger. After finishing my homework at home, I usually spend lots of my time playing with Roger.

Useful Expressions 活學活用

 情境一：自我介紹

1. I go to ABC School.
   我在 ABC 學校讀書。

2. I'm four / five / six years old.
   我四 / 五 / 六歲。

3. I was born in America.
   我在美國出生。

 情境二：介紹家人

4. There are three / four / five people in my family.
   我家裏有三 / 四 / 五個人。

5. My dad is a firefighter / chef / doctor.
   我爸爸是一個消防員 / 廚師 / 醫生。

6. I have one brother / sister.
   我有一個哥哥 / 弟弟 / 姐姐 / 妹妹。

7. I'm the oldest / youngest in the family.
   在家裏，我是最大 / 最小的孩子。

8. I'm an only child.
   我是獨生子。

西方文化 GoGoGo!

美國有許多老師會為「自我介紹」準備一個環節，叫做 Star of the Week。每個孩子都有一個屬於自己的星期，在該星期裏，這個孩子是班裏的小星星，需要當着全班介紹自己。試過幾次之後，孩子的自我介紹就非常熟練，一點都不怯場了。

 情境三：談談自己的嗜好

9. I like playing ball games / the piano.
   我喜歡打球 / 彈鋼琴。

10. I like to play with my friends.
    我喜歡和朋友一起玩。

11. I like reading / drawing a lot.
    我很喜歡閱讀 / 繪畫。

Scene 84

表示感謝

I will say thank you.
我會說謝謝。

 Conversation 美國家庭這樣說

Boy: Mom, Uncle Pang gave this to me, but I already have one!

Mom: I know you're excited about getting new things, but I want to be clear about one thing.

Boy: What is it, Mom?

Mom: When opening your gift, the polite way to respond is to say "thank you". If you open a present and say something like "I already have this" or "Why didn't I get what he got?" then I'm taking it away.

Boy: Don't worry, I will say thank you. I will!

美國父母從小就會教孩子如何對別人的善意表示感謝（Thank you），不管是家人、鄰居或是其他人，所有善意都會被熱烈地回應。

Useful Expressions 活學活用

聆聽英文內容

 ## 情境一：作出適當的提醒

1. What do we say after we get a gift?

   我們收到禮物時應該說什麼呢？

2. What do we say when someone gives us a treat?

   人家接待我們，我們該說什麼呢？

 ## 情境二：表示感謝

3. Thank you very much.

   非常感謝你。

4. I really don't know how to thank you.

   我真的不知道該怎麼感謝你。

 ## 情境三：回敬對方

5. I want to express my thanks. Here's a little present.

   我想表達我的感謝之情，這是送你的小禮物。

6. It's a thank-you note.

   這是一封感謝信。

情境四：還有很多表示感謝的情況！

7. Thank you for everything you've done for me.

   謝謝你為我做的一切。

8. Thank you for helping me.

   謝謝你的幫忙。

9. Thank you for your compliment.

   謝謝你的稱讚。

10. Please say thank you to Grandma for taking you to the park.

    祖母帶你到公園玩耍，請你跟她說謝謝。

Scene 85 不要插話

Excuse me.
不好意思。

💬 Conversation 美國家庭這樣說

Boy: Mommy! Mommy! Mommy!

Mom: Hey, if you want to get my attention right away, say "Excuse me." It's not polite to keep saying "Mommy, Mommy" over and over again.

Boy: Excuse me, Mommy.

Mom: Right. Next time, do not interrupt people who are speaking with each other unless there is an emergency. We will notice you and respond when we are finished talking. Okay?

英文能力 UP！

當你想引起他人注意或想談話，最禮貌的說法是 Excuse me.（不好意思，打擾了。）在公共場所不小心打了嗝，就得趕快說聲 Excuse me. 在擁擠的地方，想要從別人身邊擠過去，最常用的也是 Excuse me. 如果你有急事，別人聽到這句話都會自動為你讓路。

Useful Expressions 活學活用

聆聽英文內容

 情境一：不要隨便插話

1. Please don't interrupt me. I'll be finished in a minute.
   請不要打斷我，我很快就會説完。

2. I won't bother Mom while she's on the phone.
   媽媽打電話的時候，我不會騷擾她。

3. Excuse me, Mom. Can I talk to you for a minute?
   媽，不好意思。我可以跟您聊一會兒嗎？

 情境二：跟陌生人展開對話

4. Excuse me, does this bus go to Ocean Park?
   不好意思，這輛巴士去海洋公園嗎？

 情境三：表示歉意

5. Oh, you stepped on my foot!
   噢，你踩到我的腳！

6. Excuse me!
   不好意思！

英文能力 UP！

在美式英語中，如果偶然碰到某人，或踩到某人的腳，會説：Excuse me! 但在英式英語中，人們在相同的情況下會説：I'm sorry.

 情境四：讚美孩子有禮貌

7. I'm glad you remembered your good manners.
   我很高興你能保持禮貌。

8. Thank you for being polite and I'll be with you in a minute.
   謝謝你這麼有禮，我馬上就過來。

9. Thank you for waiting for me to finish. Now it's your turn.
   謝謝你讓我先説完，現在到你了。

Scene 86 排隊好習慣

Wait your turn.

得等候輪到你。

💬 Conversation 美國家庭這樣說

Boy:　Excuse me!

Mom:　No! You shouldn't cut to the front of the line. You're being rude.　趕時間

Boy:　But there're a lot of people in the line and we're in a rush, Mom.

Mom:　Even if we're in a rush, it doesn't mean we can cut in line. When there's a line, we wait our turn. Is that clear?

Boy:　Yes, I'm so sorry.

西方文化 GoGoGo!

美國有很多教導孩子遵守排隊規則的兒歌，以下這首根據 *London Bridge* 的韻律來唱的排隊歌 *Line Up*，很受美國家長和老師歡迎！

Everybody make a line, make a line, make a line.

Everybody make a line.

For now, it's (bath / lunch / etc.) time.

Useful Expressions 活學活用

 ## 情境一：一起來排隊

1. There are a lot of kids already waiting in the line.

   已經有很多小孩在排隊了。

2. I'm the first in line.

   我排在第一。

3. This line is so long!

   這條隊好長呀！

4. Let's line up nicely.

   我們好好排隊吧。

 ## 情境二：排隊時的規則

5. Be patient.

   耐心點。

6. Wait your turn.

   得等候輪到你。

7. Never push or jostle people.

   不要推擠別人。

8. I will line up for lunch / for the library / for the bus.

   我吃午飯 / 在圖書館 / 等巴士的時候會排隊。

情境三：如果有人插隊

9. Sorry, I think that I am the next in line.

   對不起，我在這兒排隊呢。

10. Please don't cut in line.

    請不要插隊。

11. Please get back into line.

    請你排隊。

Scene 87 道歉
I'm sorry.
對不起。

💬 Conversation 美國家庭這樣說

Girl: Mom! George's throwing shoes at me!

Mom: George, come out from there. I want to talk to you. George, where are you? Come over here.

Boy: She started it. She hit me first.

Mom: George, what you were doing was dangerous. Throwing anything at anybody is dangerous. Were you making fun of your sister? If you were, then please apologize.

Boy: Okay. I'm sorry.

西方文化 GoGoGo!

學會道歉,是教養的基本標準。美國家長常常告訴孩子,一句 Sorry(對不起)能改善人際關係。自己做錯了什麼,及時表示抱歉,也是有風度和教養的表現。

Useful Expressions 活學活用

聆聽英文內容

 情境一：表示道歉

1. It was my fault.

   是我的錯。

2. Forgive me, please.

   請原諒我。

3. It was a mistake.

   是我不小心。

4. I'm sorry. I'm late.

   對不起，我遲到了。

5. I didn't mean it.

   我不是故意的。

6. I didn't mean to do that.

   我不是故意這樣做。

> **英文能力 UP！**
>
> 這種表示抱歉的說法是最常見的，如果想強調抱歉的心情，那就可以說：I'm really sorry.（我真的很抱歉。）

 情境二：接受別人道歉

7. It's okay.

   沒關係。

8. No problem.

   沒關係。

9. Never mind.

   不用在意。

10. That's not a problem.

    那不是問題。

11. I'll forgive you.

    我會原諒你的。

12. It doesn't matter.

    這不要緊。

Scene
88

公眾場合的禮儀

Let me give my seat to her.
我把座位讓給她吧。

💬 **Conversation 美國家庭這樣說**

Mom: Go sit in an empty seat.

Boy: Mom, what does this big red smile on the seat stand for?

Mom: These are Priority Seats. They are reserved for the
關愛座　elderly, someone who is pregnant or anyone carrying a
baby.

Boy: I see. Here comes a woman with a baby. Let me give my
seat to her.

Mom: Awesome! You're so polite to offer your seat to someone
who is in need. I'm so proud that you behave like a big
boy!

Useful Expressions 活學活用

聆聽英文內容

 情境一：公眾場合裏的禮儀

1. We walk inside. Don't run.

   我們在室內走路，別跑。

2. Let's use our inside voices. Don't yell.

   我們說話輕聲點，不要大叫。

 情境二：有人打噴嚏時

3. Achoo!

   阿嚏！

4. Bless you.

   祝福你。

5. Thank you.

   謝謝。

西方文化 GoGoGo!

美國有句話是 Manners make the man.（教養造就人。）人們非常重視教養，在公共場合很少看到亂跑、喧嘩的孩子。如果有擾亂公共秩序的行為，大人也會馬上制止。不少美國學校有一門課叫做 Learn Polite Words（學習禮貌用語），提醒孩子做個有禮貌的人。

 情境三：進出大門時

6. Can you hold the door for Grandma?

   你可以扶着門，讓祖母先出 / 進去嗎？

7. After you.

   你先請。

 情境四：提出請求時

8. Can I have some candy?

   我可以要糖果嗎？

9. What's the magic word?

   有魔力的單詞是什麼呢？

10. Can I have some candy, please?

   請問我可以要糖果嗎？

家長手記

Please（請）被美國家長稱為 magic word（有魔力的單詞）。當孩子忘記禮貌時，家長可在旁提醒：What's the magic word? 孩子就會立刻明白該說些什麼了。

Scene 89

表達開心的情緒

I'm happy.
我很開心。

💬 Conversation 美國家庭這樣說

Mom: You look happy. Did anything funny happen?

Boy: Mom, today was a very exciting day. I'm happy my teacher praised me a lot.

Mom: What did you do that made you and your teacher so happy?

Boy: I did a good job on the test and my teacher gave me three stickers. I wish every day were like today.

Mom: That's cool. It sounds like you had a fun and interesting day.

英文能力 UP！

Sounds like（聽起來好像）後可接名詞，例如：It sounds like a dog.（聽起來像是隻狗。）也可接句子，例如：It sounds like you had an exciting day.（聽起來你好像度過了刺激的一天。）

Useful Expressions 活學活用

聆聽英文內容

 情境一：表達開心或興奮的情緒

1. How do you feel today?

   你今天覺得如何？

2. I feel great.

   我覺得很好。

3. I'm in a good mood today.

   我今天的心情很好。

4. I'm really excited about today.

   我今天真的很興奮。

5. I'm so excited that I can't even sleep.

   我太興奮了，睡不着。

6. Mommy's glad that you're happy.

   看到你開心，媽媽也很開心。

 情境二：說明開心或興奮的原因

7. I'm happy I did a good job on the test.

   我很高興我的測驗考得很好。

8. I'm happy that the vacation has started.

   我很高興假期開始了。

9. I can't wait for my birthday.

   我等不及要過生日了。

10. I can't wait for the school picnic.

    我等不及要去學校旅行了。

11. I'm glad my teacher said good things about me.

    我很高興老師讚美我。

12. I'm glad you praised me.

    我很高興你稱讚我。

Scene 90

表達傷心的情緒

You look sad. What happened?

你看來很傷心，發生了什麼事？

💬 Conversation 美國家庭這樣說

Mom: You look sad. What happened?

Girl: I'm sad because my best friend did not come to school today.

Mom: Are you talking about Irina? Why's that? Where did she go?

Girl: She's moved to another school. I'm not gonna see her again. I feel down.

Mom: Even though Irina has moved to another school, you can still see her. We may visit her on the weekend.

英文能力 UP！

Even though 的句型意指「即使、雖然」，用法與 though 或 although 相同，同樣不可與 but 並用。例如：Grandma is still very active even though she is 90.（雖然祖母已經 90 歲了，但她依然非常活躍。）

Useful Expressions 活學活用

聆聽英文內容

 情境一：表達傷心的情緒

1. I'm sad.

   我很傷心。

2. I was so sad that I cried a lot.

   我很傷心，所以我一直在哭。

3. I was so sad that I couldn't stop my tears.

   我難過得眼淚流不停。

 情境二：說出傷心的原因

4. I'm sad because my classmate lied to me.

   我感到難過是因為我的同學向我說謊。

5. I'm sad because my best friend has moved to another school.

   我感到難過是因為我最好的朋友轉校了。

6. I'm depressed because my dog died.

   我感到沮喪是因為小狗死了。

7. I'm sad because I didn't do well / did poorly on my test.

   我感到難過是因為測驗考得不好 / 考得差。

8. This is a very sad movie. It makes me cry.

   這是一部非常悲傷的電影，它讓我流淚了。

 情境三：安慰難過的孩子

9. Don't cry.

   不要哭了。

10. Don't be sad.

    不要難過。

11. Everything will be all right.

    一切會好起來的。

Scene 91 表達嫉妒的情緒
I love you both in special ways.
你們兩個我都疼愛。

💬 Conversation 美國家庭這樣說

Boy:　Mom, why did Anna get a new pair of shoes and I didn't?

Mom:　Because **hers** were worn out. 破舊

Girl:　Mom, why do I have to go to bed at 9 o'clock when George gets to stay up until 10 o'clock?

Mom:　Because you need more sleep.

Boy:　Mom, who do you love more – me or Anna?

Mom:　I love you both in special ways. You're my firstborn, and no one else can be my firstborn son.

> **英文能力 UP！**
> Hers 是 she 的第三人稱所有格代名詞（possessive pronoun），用來表示人們擁有的東西。以上 hers 代替了名詞 pair of shoes，意思是 her pair of shoes。

Useful Expressions 活學活用

聆聽英文內容

 情境一：表達嫉妒的情緒

1. Mom, why do you favor Sis over me? I feel bad.

   媽，為什麼您總是更疼愛妹妹？我很傷心。

家長手記 嫉妒有機會來自孩子內心的不安全感，父母不妨反思一下，是否平時陪伴孩子的時間不夠，或在言行上不經意間讓孩子感受到不公平的待遇。千萬別在孩子面前作出誰好誰壞的比較，例如：Why can't you make good grades like your sister / brother?（你為什麼就不能像你兄弟 / 姐妹一樣拿到好成績？）讓孩子感受到你對他獨一無二的愛，是幫助他們建立安全感，對抗嫉妒的有效方法。

 情境二：媽媽是很公平的呀！

2. I love you both the same.

   我對你們兩個的愛都是一樣的。

3. You and your sister / brother are both important to me.

   你和妹妹 / 弟弟對我來說同樣重要。

4. Come here, Mommy will give you a hug / cuddle.

   過來，媽媽給你抱抱。

5. You don't know how much Mommy loves you.

   你不知道媽媽有多愛你。

情境三：家人要相親相愛

6. Friends come and go. Brothers and sisters are forever.

   朋友有聚有散，兄弟姐妹是一生一世的。

7. Your friends may move or drift away, but your family will always be there when you need them.

   朋友會離開你，會疏遠你，但當你需要家人的時候，他們永遠會在你身邊。

Scene 92 表達失望的情緒

Suck it up, Sweetie.

小甜心，算了吧。

💬 Conversation 美國家庭這樣說

Girl: I should have been chosen as the princess in the school play!

Mom: Yes, you really should have been chosen as the beautiful princess in the school play, but unfortunately someone else was considered a little better than you and was therefore chosen instead.

Girl: I'm really disappointed.

Mom: I know. It must have made you unhappy. Suck it up, Sweetie. We may not control every bad thing that happens, but we do control how we react to those bad things.

Useful Expressions 活學活用

 情境一：表達失望的情緒

1. It's really disappointing.

   這太讓人失望了。

2. I'm really disappointed.

   我真的很失望。

 英文能力 UP！

Disappointed 用來指人，表示對某人或某事感到失望；disappointing 則用於事物給人的感覺，表示某些事情是「令人失望的」。

 情境二：說明失望的原因

3. I'm disappointed you forgot to bring any presents.

   你忘了給我帶禮物，我很失望。

4. I'm disappointed because I did not do well in the test.

   我很失望，因為測驗考得不好。

5. They didn't let me join the game.

   他們玩遊戲的時候不讓我加入。

6. They were out of my favorite dessert.

   他們沒有我最喜歡吃的甜點。

 情境三：提醒孩子不要氣餒

7. Don't feel so bad.

   不要失望。

8. You've done well by trying hard, and it's okay to make mistakes.

   你已經盡力做好了，做錯了也沒什麼大不了。

9. Don't give up, but keep on trying.

   不要放棄，繼續努力。

10. Let's see if we can find something good in this.

    我們看看有什麼得着。

11. It's okay. You are making progress.

    不要緊的，你已有進步了。

Scene 93

表達驚慌的情緒

I had a nightmare.

我發了個噩夢。

 Conversation 美國家庭這樣說

Mom: You said something in your sleep last night. You sounded very frightened.

Boy: Really? What did I say?

Mom: I think you said, "Get out of here! Help! Help!"

Boy: Oh, I can remember now. I think I had a nightmare.

Mom: What did you dream about?

Boy: I saw a monster. I was so scared!

家長手記

Help! 是遇到危險時，用作呼救的話，意為：來人啊！救命啊！家長可教導兒女這樣做：Yell for help! Make a lot of noise if you're scared.（大叫救命！害怕時就大聲叫。）

Useful Expressions 活學活用

聆聽英文內容

 ## 情境一：表達驚慌的情緒

1. I'm scared.
   我很害怕。
2. It's creepy.
   這令人毛骨悚然。
3. I'm shivering.
   我在發抖。

 ## 情境二：説出驚慌的原因

4. I'm afraid of the dark.
   我怕黑。
5. I'm scared to stay at home alone.
   我害怕一個人待在家裏。
6. I'm afraid of spiders / cockroaches.
   我害怕蜘蛛 / 蟑螂。
7. The ghosts / monsters in the horror movie are scary.
   恐怖電影裏的鬼 / 怪獸很可怕。

 ## 情境三：鼓勵孩子要堅強呀！

8. Don't be scared, Sweetie.
   不用怕，小甜心。
9. You don't need to be afraid.
   你不需要害怕。
10. Be brave / strong!
    拿出勇氣 / 要堅強！
11. Hold me so that I don't get scared.
    抱着我，我就不會害怕了。

Scene 94

表達生氣的情緒

What bugs you at school today?

今天學校發生了什麼事讓你生氣？

💬 Conversation 美國家庭這樣說

Mom: Why are you angry? What bugs you at school today?

Boy: Martin's picking his nose.

Mom: That's pretty gross, but it's his nose.

Boy: He wiped the boogers on my clothes. I feel angry.

Mom: We can let his parents take care of it. Thank you for telling me.

英文能力 UP！

形容詞 gross 用於口語，指「令人討厭的」東西，例如：Oh, gross! I hate cockroaches!（噢，噁心！我討厭蟑螂！）gross 也可作動詞，與 out 連用，指「使人作嘔」。例如：His dirty fingernails really gross me out!（他的髒指甲真的讓我感到噁心！）

Useful Expressions 活學活用

聆聽英文內容

 情境一：詢問生氣的原因

1. What made you that mad?
   是什麼讓你那麼生氣？

2. Why are you in a bad mood today? What's wrong?
   為什麼你今天心情這麼差？有什麼事？

3. Anybody get on your nerves today?
   有誰惹怒了你嗎？

 情境二：說明生氣的原因

4. I get annoyed by my friend.
   我被我的朋友惹怒了。

5. My friend didn't keep his promise. That makes me angry.
   我的朋友沒有遵守諾言，這讓我很生氣。

6. My friend screamed at me.
   我的朋友向我大吼大叫。

7. My classmate hit me.
   我的同學打我。

 情境三：學習控制脾氣

8. I'm so angry that I can't calm down.
   我太生氣了，無法冷靜下來。

9. Calm down.
   冷靜點。

10. Get over it.
    鎮定一下。

11. You need to deal with your temper.
    你需要管理你的情緒。

Scene 95

打電話
Who are you calling, please?
請問你要找哪位？

💬 Conversation 美國家庭這樣說

Girl: Mom, the phone is ringing.

Mom: Mom's in the kitchen. Will you pick up the phone for me?

Girl: Okay, I'll get it. Hello, who are you calling, please?
Mom, it's for Dad!

Mom: Ask who's calling and Dad will call them back when he gets home.

Girl: Okay.

西方文化 GoGoGo!

在美國拿起電話後，要先說 Hello / Good morning / Good afternoon，給對方一點時間預備對話。提及自己時不要說 "I am..."，應該說 "This is..." 或 "That's me."，例如：This is George.（我是佐治。）

202

Useful Expressions 活學活用

 情境一：打電話

1. Hello, this is Anna. May I please speak to Colin?

   嗨，我是安娜。我可以跟葛林説話嗎？

2. Hi, Colin, this is Anna. Is your sister in?

   嗨，葛林，我是安娜。你妹妹在嗎？

3. I will call him / her again later then. Thank you.

   我稍後再給他 / 她打電話吧，謝謝。

 情境二：接電話

4. Who is speaking, please?

   請問你是誰？

5. Who would you like to speak to?

   你要找哪位？

6. This is she / he.

   我就是。

7. He's / She's out.

   他 / 她出去了。

8. It's for you, Mom.

   媽，這是找您的。

9. Just a moment, please. / Hold the line, please.

   請等一下。

西方文化 GoGoGo!

美國人接到打錯了的電話，一般會説：I'm sorry. I'm afraid you've got the wrong number. （抱歉，恐怕你打錯電話了。）

 情境三：爸爸媽媽不在家時

10. Mom's not here. Can I take a message?

    媽媽不在，你要留個口訊嗎？

11. Can I please have my mom / dad call you back later?

    我叫媽媽 / 爸爸稍後給你回電話好嗎？

Scene 96

喜好和夢想

My hobby is to play the piano.

我的嗜好是彈鋼琴。

💬 Conversation 美國家庭這樣說

Mom: Hey Sweetie, I brought you some DVDs.

Boy: Thank you but watching movies is not really a hobby for me.

Mom: Oh! I thought you would like them. What do you like to do in your spare time then?

Boy: My hobby is to play the piano. I can play for hours. I want to be a pianist when I grow up.

家長手記

家長可以問：What do you want to be when you grow up?（你長大了想做什麼？）來詢問孩子的志向，而孩子一般可回答：I want to be a teacher / doctor / etc.（我想當老師 / 醫生。）

Useful Expressions 活學活用

 情境一：談興趣和喜好

1. What are your hobbies?

   你有什麼嗜好？

2. My hobby is reading / playing badminton.

   我的嗜好是看書 / 打羽毛球。

3. I really enjoy drawing.

   我真的很喜歡繪畫。

 情境二：擅長做的事情

4. I am good at swimming / making crafts.

   我擅長游泳 / 做手工藝。

5. My music teacher said I have a good ear for music.

   我的音樂老師說我有音樂天分。

6. My art teacher said I have a talent for art.

   我的美術老師說我有藝術天分。

 情境三：談夢想和志願

7. My dream is to be a singer / an astronaut.

   我的夢想是成為一個歌手 / 太空人。

8. I want to be a doctor / lawyer.

   我想成為一個醫生 / 律師。

9. I love dancing, so I want to be a dancer.

   我喜歡跳舞，所以我想成為一個舞蹈員。

10. Although I like sports, I want to be a teacher when I grow up.

    雖然我喜歡運動，不過我希望長大以後能成為一個老師。

11. I want to be a writer like Dad.

    我想跟爸爸一樣，成為一個作家。

Scene 97 勝出比賽
Yay! Here's the winner!
耶！優勝者來了！

💬 Conversation 美國家庭這樣說

Boy: Mom, I scored a goal at soccer today.

Mom: You scored a goal. Fantastic!

Boy: And our team won the championship!

Mom: Yay! Here's the winner! Let me see the medal. Awesome!
Are you proud of yourself? You should be.

Boy: I feel great!

Mom: I feel proud of you, Sweetie. Let's call Daddy and tell him
the good news!

英文能力 UP！

感歎詞 Yay!（耶！/ 吔！）用來表達滿意或非常高興的心情。其他表示高興
的呼喊聲還有 Hooray!（太棒！/ 好哇！）和 Woo-hoo!（哇哈！/ 哦呵！）

Useful Expressions 活學活用

聆聽英文內容

 情境一：勝出比賽

1. Mom, I won a prize!
   媽，我得獎了！

2. I won the gold medal!
   我拿到了金牌！

3. Mom, I'm the champ today!
   媽，今天我是冠軍！

英文能力 UP！

Champ 是 champion（冠軍）的非正式說法，常用於口語或在報章裏使用。

 情境二：獲獎感受

4. Hooray! You made it! How do you feel?
   太棒了！你成功了！你感覺怎樣？

5. I feel great / terrific!
   我覺得很棒！

家長手記

美國家長往往避免以物質獎勵孩子，反而以榮耀感、成就感、自主選擇（freedom of choice）等驅動孩子，讓他們感受到自己的努力獲得認同。

 情境三：表示恭喜

6. Super game! Congratulations!
   很精彩的比賽！恭喜！

7. You won first place! You impress me.
   你拿到了第一名！真讓我佩服。

8. Let's give a round of applause!
   大家拍手鼓掌！

 情境四：給予支持或獎勵

9. Let's go to the park to celebrate.
   我們去公園慶祝一下吧。

10. Well done! You can choose what we have for dessert.
    做得非常好！由你來決定我們吃什麼甜品吧。

Scene 98

完成任務
Two thumbs up!
給你兩個讚！

💬 **Conversation 美國家庭這樣說**

Girl: Mom, I am so happy that I can write from A to Z.

Mom: That's great!

Girl: Did I do well, Mom?

Mom: **Two thumbs up!** You did so well. All your letters are right between the lines. I'll bet your teacher won't have any trouble reading this.

Girl: I'm going to try harder next time.

Mom: Super! You're such an amazing girl!

家長手記

家長可以用 Two thumbs up! 來稱讚孩子做得很好，說話時還要豎起兩隻大拇指來配合意思。其他稱讚說法還包括：Nicely done! / Good job! / Awesome! / Amazing!

Useful Expressions 活學活用

聆聽英文內容

 情境一：完成任務了

1. I can make it.
   我成功了。

2. I did it all by myself.
   我是自己一個人完成的。

 情境二：獲得嘉許

3. I got a good manners award.
   我得到了好禮貌獎。

4. My teacher gave me a praise sticker today.
   今天老師給我一張獎勵貼紙。

5. I got a sticker because I answered a question correctly.
   我答對了題目,所以得到一張貼紙。

 情境三：稱讚孩子

6. You're so smart!
   你真聰明!

7. Just fantastic!
   了不起!

 情境四：建立孩子的自信

8. Look at your improvement!
   你進步了!

9. You've done really well at school.
   你在學校的表現真的很好。

10. You just proved to yourself that you should never give up.
    你剛向自己證明了,只要不放棄就行。

 家長手記

在孩提時累積成就感,是孩子養成自信心(self-confidence)的重要過程。家長可從生活上的一些小事為孩子設定目標,留意目標不一定要遠大,但必須讓孩子能夠達到,從而逐步建立他們的自信。

Scene 99

學會分享

We are supposed to share.
我們必須互相分享。

💬 Conversation 美國家庭這樣説

Mom: Anna, please give some of the cookies to George.

Girl: No.

Mom: We are supposed to share with our family.

Girl: I don't like to share.

Mom: Look, this teddy bear says that he doesn't want to share with his sister. How do you think his sister feels? What should we tell this silly teddy bear?

Girl: We should tell him to…hmm, share please.

西方文化 GoGoGo!

美國有句諺語叫 Sharing is caring（分享是福）。
在美國，學會與他人分享是小孩從小就得學習的
美德，也是重要的社交能力（social skill）之一。

Useful Expressions 活學活用

聆聽英文內容

 情境一：分享的意義

1. Sharing spreads joy.
   分享能給別人帶來快樂。

2. We need to share with each other.
   我們必須互相分享。

 情境二：學習分享

3. Want some of my cookies?
   你要吃我的甜餅乾嗎？

4. Let's share this banana. You can have some, and I can have some.
   我們把這香蕉分來吃吧。這是你的，這是我的。

5. Now it's my turn to play, then it's your turn.
   現在我先來玩，然後到你。

6. You share the yellow blocks with me, and I'll share the red blocks with you.
   你分一些黃色積木給我，我分一些紅色積木給你。

7. When I am all done with the bicycle, then you can ride it.
   我先騎這腳踏車，然後到你騎。

 情境三：希望別人也能分享

8. Let's play together, okay?
   我們一起玩，好不好？

9. When will be my turn?
   什麼時候輪到我？

10. It's my turn now. We play together because we are good friends.
    現在該輪到我了，我們是好朋友，所以一起玩。

Scene 100 愛護大自然

Now it's time to let them go!
是時候讓牠們走了！

💬 **Conversation 美國家庭這樣說**

Boy: Mom, look here! What a fat, wiggly worm!

Mom: It's a caterpillar. See how cute it is. Look, there are a few more here. How many are there?

Boy: I see five. They're making their way up the branch. Let me poke them with a stick.

Mom: Oh no! You shouldn't do that. They're now going home. Now it's time to let them go!

家長手記 美國作家理查‧洛夫（Richard Louv）呼籲家長讓孩子親近大自然，透過自然讓孩子獲得正能量。這樣能減輕他們專注力失調及過度活躍症（ADHD）的症狀，並改善認知能力，以及面對壓力和抑鬱的抵抗能力。

Useful Expressions 活學活用

聆聽英文內容

 情境一：愛護大自然

1. Don't pick the flowers.
   不可以摘花。

2. Don't throw pebbles at the birds.
   不可以向鳥兒拋石頭。

 情境二：培養同理心

3. When you hurt a flower / butterfly, you hurt its feelings and growth.
   如果你傷害了花朵 / 蝴蝶，你會讓它們 / 牠們傷心，妨礙生長。

4. Things need to grow. Let's be gentle.
   它們 / 牠們需要成長，我們要溫柔點。

5. What if every kid picked a flower? What would the park really turn into?
   要是每個孩子都摘一朵花，這個公園會變成怎樣呢？

 情境三：做個好孩子

6. I won't step on the grass.
   我不會踐踏草地。

7. I won't pick the flowers.
   我不會摘花。

8. I won't break the branches.
   我不會折斷樹枝。

9. I won't hurt the small animals.
   我不會傷害小動物。

10. I won't litter.
   我不會隨地扔垃圾。

Scene 101

説謊
In our home, we tell the truth.
在這個家，我們都説實話。

💬 Conversation 美國家庭這樣説

Mom: Sweetie, you need to make your bed.

Girl: I DID it already!

Mom: No, you didn't. Your bed looks so messy. Maybe you thought you made your bed?

Girl: No, I actually did it.

Mom: I'm sorry, but you're not being honest. To say you made the bed when it is obvious that you didn't is not telling the truth. In our home, we tell the truth.

家長手記

家長發現孩子説謊時，盡量不要大加責備説：You lie! You're a bad kid!（你説謊！你是個壞孩子！）因為這樣反而讓孩子更不敢説實話。要了解孩子究竟為何要説謊，才能有效解決問題。

Useful Expressions 活學活用

id="2" /> 聆聽英文內容

 情境一：說謊讓人心痛

1. Why did you lie?

   你為什麼説謊？

2. Mommy's upset because you lied.

   因為你説謊，媽媽很不開心。

3. Lying is wrong, it's hurtful.

   説謊是錯的，説謊會傷害別人。

 情境二：誠實是一種美德

4. Honesty is important.

   誠實是很重要的。

家長手記

當孩子承認撒謊，表示今後會改正時，家長必須相信他，讓孩子受到鼓舞，徹底改掉撒謊的毛病。

 情境三：承認錯誤

5. I'm sorry that I lied.

   對不起，我説謊了。

6. I lied because I was afraid you would scold me.

   我害怕你會責備我，所以才説謊。

7. I won't scold you, so tell me the truth.

   我不責備你，告訴我實話。

8. It's brave to tell the truth.

   説實話是很有勇氣的。

 情境四：以後不再説謊了

9. Mommy trusts you. You won't do it again, right?

   媽媽相信你，你不會再這樣做，對吧？

10. I won't do it again.

    我再也不會説謊了。

215

吵架和打架

Hitting is not okay.
打人是不對的。

Conversation 美國家庭這樣說

Mom: Look at your sister – she's very sad. She's crying. She's rubbing her arm where you pushed her. Why did you do that?

Boy: She took my toy away! And she yelled at me.

Mom: But hitting is not okay, no matter how upset you are. Remember how sad you were when your friend yelled at you? That might be how your sister feels now.

Boy: I won't ever fight again.

Mom: Okay. Say sorry to each other. Next time, let's not hit our brother or sister. We don't want to hurt them.

Useful Expressions 活學活用

聆聽英文內容

 ## 情境一：吵架的原因

1. Why did you fight?

   你們為什麼吵架？

2. We both wanted the same toy.

   我們都想要同一個玩具。

3. He / She took my toy away.

   他 / 她搶了我的玩具。

4. He / She yelled at me.

   他 / 她對我大吼大叫。

5. He / She kept hitting me.

   他 / 她一直打我。

 ## 情境二：指出錯誤

6. There are manners to keep even among brothers and sisters.

   即使是兄弟姐妹，也要保持禮貌。

7. No hitting your sister / brother.

   不要打你的姐妹 / 兄弟。

8. We use our words, not our hands.

   我們用口講道理，不用手。

 ## 情境三：向對方道歉

9. Say sorry to your sister / brother.

   跟你的姐妹 / 兄弟說對不起。

10. I'm sorry. It's my fault.

    對不起，是我的錯。

11. I didn't mean to do that. Please forgive me.

    我不是故意的，請原諒我。

Scene
103

發脾氣
Where are your manners?
你的禮貌呢？

 Conversation 美國家庭這樣說

Mom: I'm really sorry but we have to go now. I see you're upset. I hear that you want to stay, but it is dinner time and we're leaving now.

Girl: Waa…waa…wa…! No! No! No! I'm playing on the swing.

Mom: You're having so much fun on the swing. But we need to go home now.

Girl: Go away!

Mom: Where are your manners? Okay, Sweetie, I see it's too hard for you to leave the swing yourself. Let's sit for a minute on the board. I'll hold you while you cry.

Useful Expressions 活學活用

聆聽英文內容

 情境一：孩子大發脾氣時

1. Don't shout! That's not polite.
   不要大叫！那是沒禮貌。

2. I hate being pushed. I really want you to stop pushing me.
   我討厭被人推撞，我希望你不要再推撞我。

 情境二：以同理心處理問題

3. Why are you taking out your anger?
   你為什麼要發脾氣？

4. Mom, you don't understand!
   媽，您不會明白的！

5. I've had a bad day.
   我今天過得很糟糕。

6. I understand, but what can you do instead of yelling at me?
   我明白，但你非要對着我大吼大叫嗎？

7. I'm sorry. I just couldn't control myself.
   對不起，我一時控制不住情緒。

家長手記

孩子犯了錯，必須承擔責任與後果。Time out（獨處）是美國家長常用的教育方式。當孩子發脾氣亂丟東西，或搶玩具時，家長就會下令：You need a time out!

 情境三：給予孩子冷靜與反思的空間

8. We are not staying here. We can come back when you can pull yourself together. We are leaving now.
   我們不能再留在這裏，你控制好情緒的話我們就會回來，我們現在要走了。

9. Go to your room! You need a time out!
   回去你的房間！你得獨處了 / 你不能再玩了！

Scene 104

壞習慣

You shouldn't do that again.
你不應該再這樣做。

💬 Conversation 美國家庭這樣說

Mom: Don't wipe your nose on your sleeve.

Boy: But I don't have tissue.

Mom: Then go get a tissue in the bathroom.

Boy: I didn't have time to get one from there.

Mom: Your sleeves are not tissues.

Boy: But Mom, all my friends use their sleeves.

Mom: That doesn't make it right. You shouldn't do that again.

家長手記

不論好習慣還是壞習慣，兒時一旦形成，往往會伴隨一生。
作為孩子第一位老師，家長需要在日常生活中多培養孩子的
好習慣，發現並及時改掉他們的壞習慣。

Useful Expressions 活學活用

聆聽英文內容

 情境一：指出壞習慣的不良影響

1. Who put this booger here? It's so dirty!

   是誰把鼻屎沾在這裏的？這很髒！

2. Don't suck your thumb. Germs will get into your body.

   不要吮大拇指，細菌會進入你的身體裏去。

3. Close the door when you poop. It stinks!

   大便的時候把門關上，很臭啊！

4. Why is there water / milk on the floor? Do you want to cause a slip and fall accident?

   為什麼地上會有水 / 奶？你想看到有滑倒的意外發生嗎？

5. No biting. Biting hurts.

   別咬人，咬人會讓人受傷的。

6. Trim your fingernails / toenails. They are too long / dirty.

   修剪一下你的手指甲 / 腳趾甲吧，太長 / 髒了。

7. Could you please wash your hands before dinner? You can help yourself and others stay healthy.

   你在吃晚飯前可以先洗洗手嗎？這能讓你和大家保持健康。

情境二：改掉壞習慣，做個有修養的孩子

8. I will not pick my nose in front of people.

   我不會在別人面前挖鼻孔了。

9. I won't wipe my nose on my sleeve.

   我不會用衣袖擦鼻子了。

10. I won't bite my fingernails.

    我不會咬手指了。

11. I'll cover my mouth with my hand when I sneeze.

    我打噴嚏的時候會用手捂着嘴巴。

Scene 105

感冒

I don't feel well.

我覺得不舒服。

 Conversation 美國家庭這樣說

Mom: What's wrong? You don't look so good.

Boy: I don't feel well. I feel cold.

Mom: Oh dear, you're shivering. I think you caught a cold at the ice rink yesterday.

Boy: Do I need to go to school today?

Mom: No, you can't go to school. Stay in bed. Let me make you some tea. It may help you feel better.

英文能力 UP！

Oh dear! 或 Dear me! 用來表示驚訝、困惑、同情等（多為女性用語），意思是「哎呀！／天呀！」如有人說：My daughter is ill again.（我女兒又病了。）就可以回答：Oh dear! I'm sorry to hear that.（哎呀！聽到這消息讓我很難過。）

Useful Expressions 活學活用

聆聽英文內容

 情境一：患感冒了

1. Mom, I don't feel well today.
   媽，我今天覺得不舒服。

2. I feel cold and shaky.
   我覺得冷到發抖。

3. Oh, you're shivering.
   噢，你在發抖。

4. You seem to have caught a cold.
   你好像感冒了。

 情境二：感冒的症狀

5. I feel tired.
   我覺得很累。

6. I have a sore throat.
   我喉嚨痛。

7. I have a runny nose.
   我流鼻水了。

8. I have a stuffy nose.
   我鼻塞了。

9. My throat hurts when I swallow.
   我吞東西時喉嚨很痛。

10. I don't want to eat because my throat hurts.
    我喉嚨很痛，不想吃東西。

西方文化 GoGoGo!

在美國，醫生很少開抗生素（antibiotics）給患感冒的孩子服用，一般建議孩子多喝水，並採取溫水擦浴等物理降溫的方法。

 情境三：要注意休息

11. Rest will help your body get better.
    休息會讓你的身體恢復過來。

Scene

106

咳嗽

You're coughing all night.

你整晚都在咳嗽。

💬 Conversation 美國家庭這樣說

Girl: (Ahem!) Cough! Cough!　　咳嗽時發出的聲音

Mom: Oh dear, you have a bad cough.

Girl: I can't stop coughing. Cough! Cough!

Mom: Yes, you were coughing all night.

Girl: I want it to go away.

Mom: What about a cup of warm lemon water with honey? It is good for coughs.

西方文化 GoGoGo!

在美國，孩子入學後第一堂行為禮貌課上，必定會教孩子 Cover your nose when you sneeze.（打噴嚏時要擋住鼻子），這是美國公共場所約定俗成的規矩。

Useful Expressions 活學活用

聆聽英文內容

 情境一：咳嗽的時候

1. I'm coughing a lot.
   我一直在咳嗽。

2. You're coughing too hard.
   你咳得很嚴重。

3. I have some phlegm in my throat.
   我的喉嚨裏有痰。

4. My snot is yellow.
   我的鼻涕是黃色的。

家長手記

美國有研究指出：對 1 歲以上的孩子來説，蜂蜜（honey）比一般止咳藥效果更好。

 情境二：注意衞生

5. To avoid spreading germs, cover your mouth and nose when you sneeze.
   打噴嚏時擋住嘴巴和鼻子，避免細菌散播。

6. I will use a tissue or my handkerchief when I sneeze or cough.
   打噴嚏或咳嗽時我會使用紙巾或手巾。

7. Let me put the used tissue in the waste basket.
   我把用過的紙巾扔在廢紙箱裏。

8. Try not to cough on people.
   試着不要對着別人咳嗽。

9. Turn your face away.
   別過頭去。

 情境三：舒緩咳嗽的方法

10. Let's take some honey. It will calm your cough.
    我們來吃一點蜂蜜吧，這會舒緩你的咳嗽。

Scene 107

發燒
Let's check your temperature.
我們來量一下體溫。

💬 Conversation 美國家庭這樣說

Mom: What's the matter?

Girl: I think I'm just tired.

Mom: You're sweating. Oh, your forehead is hot. And your body, too.
Let's check your temperature. Oh dear, you have a fever.

Girl: Why do I get a fever?

Mom: Some germs might have got into your body and made you sick.
Your body is fighting the germs right now.

家長手記

孩子不舒服的時候，家長一般會問：What's the matter?（你怎麼啦？）其他常用的表達方法還有：What's wrong with you? / Is anything wrong? / What's the problem?

Useful Expressions 活學活用

聆聽英文內容

 情境一：感覺發燒了

1. Mom, I feel very hot.

   媽，我覺得很熱。

2. My forehead is really hot.

   我的額頭真的很燙。

3. I feel dizzy.

   我感覺頭暈。

 情境二：測量體溫

4. Let me check your temperature.

   我來量一下你的體溫。

5. Let me see if you have a fever.

   我來看看你是否發燒了。

6. Let me feel your forehead.

   我來摸一下你的額頭。

7. You have a fever, so your body feels really hot.

   你發燒了，所以身體會發熱。

 家長手記

發燒是身體受到細菌侵入而引發的症狀（symptom），人體的正常溫度是 36.5°C，小朋友的體溫通常會高一些，但若超過 37.5°C，就可能真的發燒了。

 情境三：減輕病情

8. You need to drink a lot of water.

   你要多喝一點水。

9. I'll cool you down with a wet towel.

   我用濕毛巾來幫你降溫。

10. Let's take a fever reducer.

    來吃退燒藥吧。

Scene 108

肚子痛
I have diarrhea.
我拉肚子了。

💬 Conversation 美國家庭這樣說

Mom: What's wrong with you?

Boy: Ouch, the pain in my stomach is killing me!

Mom: You have an attack of diarrhea. Did you wash your hands before eating?

Boy: No, I didn't.

Mom: Our hands touch many things in a day, so they attract a lot of germs which are invisible to the eye. These germs may cause you to have a stomachache and diarrhea.

Boy: Ouch, I've got to go to the toilet again.

英文能力 UP！

is / are killing me 用於口語，指「痛得要命」，例如：I've walked miles and my feet are killing me.（我走了很多路，腳痛得要命。）

Useful Expressions 活學活用

 情境一：拉肚子了

1. Mom, I have a stomachache.
   媽，我肚子痛。

2. My poop's coming out like water.
   我的大便像水一樣流出來。

3. I need to use the toilet again.
   我需要再去廁所了。

4. It looks like you've got an upset stomach.
   看來你鬧肚子了。

5. Do you need to poop?
   你要去大便嗎？

 情境二：拉肚子的原因

6. Mom, why do I have diarrhea?
   媽，我為什麼會拉肚子？

7. There must be something wrong with the food you have eaten.
   那一定是你吃了一些有問題的食物。

8. Do you wash your hands before you eat? You never know if you have previously touched something which may contain germs.
   你吃東西前有洗手嗎？你不會知道之前是不是接觸過什麼有細菌的東西。

情境三：舒緩肚子痛的方法

9. Mom, I want a hot pack on my tummy.
   媽，我想把熱水袋放在肚子上。

10. Let me rub your tummy. You'll be fine soon.
   我來按摩你的肚子，你很快就會好起來的。

看醫生

How does it look, doctor?
醫生，怎麼樣了？

💬 Conversation 美國家庭這樣說

Doctor: What's the problem?

Girl: I have a sore throat and a slight fever.

Doctor: Let's have a look. I need your dress off so I can listen to your chest. Can I help you take it off?

Mom: How does it look, doctor?

Doctor: Don't worry. It's nothing serious. It's an infection. I'll give you a shot.

Girl: Will it hurt?

Doctor: No. You'll be fine.

英文能力 UP！

Don't worry. 用來安慰別人，期望對方「別怕、別急、不用擔心」。

Useful Expressions 活學活用

聆聽英文內容

 情境一：覺得身體不舒服

1. I feel sick / weak.
   我覺得生病了 / 很虛弱。

2. I feel a pain in my chest / leg / waist / neck / etc.
   我的胸口 / 腿 / 腰 / 脖子痛。

3. I have a headache / stomachache.
   我頭痛 / 肚子痛。

4. I can't sleep because I'm coughing a lot.
   我一直咳嗽，睡不着。

5. I threw up everything I ate.
   我把所有吃下去的東西都吐出來了。

 情境二：接受醫生檢查和治療

6. Let's go to see a doctor.
   我們去看醫生吧。

7. Show your tongue to the doctor. Stick out your tongue.
   給醫生看看你的舌頭，把舌頭伸出來。

8. Take a deep breath. The doctor will check your lungs.
   深呼吸一下，醫生要檢查你的肺部。

 情境三：孩子害怕時

9. Do I have to get a shot?
   我要打針嗎？

10. It will sting a little. Don't be scared.
    會有一點刺痛，不用害怕。

11. Good girl / boy, you're doing well by not crying.
    做得好，你沒有哭，表現很好。

Scene 110

吃藥

How often do I take this medicine?
我要吃多少次藥？

💬 **Conversation 美國家庭這樣說**

Boy: Mom, how often do I take this medicine?

Mom: You must take it three times a day.

Boy: Three times!?

Mom: Yes. Take this dose now, and the second at around 3 pm and the third at night before sleeping.

Boy: I don't feel like taking it.

Mom: It will make you feel better. Now, you need to rest and you shouldn't worry. You'll soon be well again.

英文能力 UP！

do not feel like doing something 指沒有心情去做某事。例如：I don't feel like doing anything.（我提不起精神來做事。）

Useful Expressions 活學活用

 情境一:生病時要吃藥

1. Here, take this medicine.
   來,吃這些藥。

2. Will this make me feel better?
   我吃了會舒服點嗎?

3. Shake well before use.
   吃藥前要搖勻。

4. Swallow it. Don't spit it out.
   吞下去,不要吐出來。

 情境二:不願吃藥時

5. I hate taking medicine.
   我討厭吃藥。

6. It tastes bitter.
   它的味道很苦。

7. It makes me feel drowsy all day.
   它讓我一整天都昏昏欲睡。

8. Take these strong pills. They will make you well again.
   吃了這些威力強勁的藥,就會讓你好起來。

9. Okay, let's mix the medicine into the juice.
   好,我們把藥混進果汁裏吧。

10. If you get better, we will be able to have your friends over for a party.
    只要你康復過來,我們就可以邀請你的朋友來開派對。

 情境三:吃藥後要注意休息

11. Drink plenty of fluids and try to rest as much as you can.
    多喝些水,盡量多休息。

Scene 111

蛀牙了

You need to see a dentist.
你要去看牙醫。

💬 Conversation 美國家庭這樣說

Boy:　Oh no! Why do I have a toothache?

Mom:　Let me have a look. Open your mouth. Oh dear, I think one of your teeth is decayed. Tomorrow I'm going to take you to the dentist.

Boy:　No! I'm really afraid of going to see the dentist. I don't want to have my tooth pulled out!

Mom:　If you have a decayed tooth, you'd better go to the dentist.

英文能力 UP！

You'd better（你最好）是 You had better 的省略形式，用於提議，表示對方應該做些什麼。例如：I think you'd better ask your mom first.（我想你最好先問一下你媽媽。）

Useful Expressions 活學活用

聆聽英文內容

 情境一：牙痛了

1. What's the matter with your teeth?
   你的牙齒怎麼回事？

2. My tooth starts hurting.
   我的牙齒開始痛了。

3. I've got a pain in my back teeth.
   我的大牙痛。

4. I feel a pain in my gum.
   我感到牙肉痛。

 情境二：有蛀牙嗎？

5. Are any of my teeth decayed?
   我的牙齒壞掉了嗎？

6. There's a bit of a cavity and you're going to need a filling.
   你有些蛀牙了，需要去補牙。

 情境三：在牙科診所裏

7. Lie back and the dentist will have a good look round.
   躺下來，牙醫會幫你好好檢查。

8. Open your mouth as wide as you can.
   盡量把口張開。

9. The doctor starts extracting my tooth now.
   醫生現在開始替我拔牙。

10. Keep quite still and try to relax.
    別動，盡量放鬆身體。

11. It's done. The decayed tooth has been extracted.
    完成了，你的蛀牙已經拔出來了。

Scene 112

預防疾病

Get more exercise.

多做一些運動。

💬 Conversation 美國家庭這樣説

Girl: Mom, I'm always sick lately. What's the best way to stay healthy?

Mom: Get more exercise.

Girl: How does it work?

Mom: When you exercise, you're helping to build a strong body that will be able to move around and do all the things you need it to do. Try to be active every day and your body will thank you later.

Girl: That's easier said than done. I'm always lazy.

Mom: You should think positive! Just try!

Useful Expressions 活學活用

 情境一：你喜歡運動嗎？

1. I like to play sports.
   我喜歡體育運動。

2. I'm not good at sports.
   我不擅長體育運動。

3. What kind of sports do you like?
   你喜歡哪種體育運動？

4. What's your favorite sport?
   你最喜歡的體育運動是什麼？

情境二：一起來運動吧！

5. I want to try dancing.
   我想試試跳舞。

6. I like swimming.
   我喜歡游泳。

7. I can do push-ups.
   我可以做掌上壓。

8. Badminton and table tennis are my favorite sports.
   我最喜歡的運動是羽毛球和乒乓球。

美國一項研究顯示，有三成美國兒童的體重過重（overweight）。造成他們肥胖的主要原因是吃過多食物，尤其是垃圾食物（junk food），並且缺乏運動。

情境三：運動的好處

9. Working out makes you stronger.
   運動使人強壯。

10. Your heart is a muscle. It works hard, pumping blood every day of your life. You can help this important muscle get stronger by doing exercise.
    心臟是一塊肌肉，無時無刻努力地傳送血液。你多做運動，就能幫助這塊重要的肌肉變得強壯。

237

Scene 113

發生火警

What if there's a fire in our building?

如果我們的大廈發生火警怎麼辦？

💬 Conversation 美國家庭這樣說

Mom: What if there's a fire in our building? Would you know what to do?

Boy: Run!

Mom: Yes, the idea is to get out of the burning building quickly and safely.

Boy: Is there a plan in order not to get hurt and burnt?

Mom: Yes. If you smell fire, crawl on the floor to safety. If the door feels warm, do not open it. If possible, cover your head and neck with a wet towel.

你知道西方國家的求救電話號碼嗎？美國和加拿大是 911，英國是 999（跟香港相同），而歐盟的國際求救電話號碼是 112。

Useful Expressions 活學活用

聆聽英文內容

 ## 情境一：一旦發生火警

1. What if I see smoke coming under the door?

   如果我看到門底冒煙，那怎麼辦？

2. Don't open it!

   不要開門！

3. What if there's no smoke?

   如果沒有煙呢？

4. If there's no smoke or heat when you open the door, go go go!

   開門時看不到煙，又感覺不到熱力，那就走走走！

5. What if there's fire or smoke blocking my way out?

   如果有火或煙擋住我的去路呢？

6. Grab some wet cloth or towel and place it over your mouth to keep from breathing in the smoke.

   找一塊濕布或毛巾捂住嘴巴，避免吸入濃煙。

 ## 情境二：謹記保持冷靜

7. That's scary, Mom.

   媽，那很可怕。

8. Even if you're scared, never hide under the bed or in a closet, because the firemen will have a hard time finding you.

   即使你很害怕，也別躲在牀底或櫃子裏，這是因為消防員很難找到你。

情境三：學會求救

9. Yell for help. You can do this from an open window.

   大叫救命，你可以向着窗外大叫。

10. Call 999 if you have a phone with you.

    你手上有電話的話就撥打 999。

Scene 114

交通安全
Let's cross safely.
過馬路,要安全。

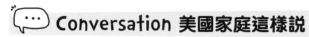

💬 Conversation 美國家庭這樣說

Mom: Let's cross safely. First check the signal — it shows the person walking, so we can cross. Now we look left, then right, then left again. Any cars?

Girl: No. No cars.

Mom: Okay, now we can cross! And your hand (is glued to) Mom.　黏住

Girl: Mommy, if I'm playing and my ball rolls into the middle of the road, what should I do?

Mom: You can ask an adult for help.

家長手記

美國家長帶孩子外出時,或在擠迫的地方都會囑咐一句:And your hand is glued to Daddy / Mommy. 這句話的意思是叫孩子緊緊地牽着爸爸 / 媽媽的手,半步也不要走開。

Useful Expressions 活學活用

聆聽英文內容

 情境一：注意交通安全

1. Mom, the light is green. Let's go.

   媽，綠燈了，我們走吧。

2. Hold my hand and walk.

   牽着我的手走。

3. Watch out! Be careful of the cars.

   小心！小心有汽車。

4. I'm fine, Mom.

   媽，我沒事。

> **英文能力 UP！**
>
> Crosswalk 是美式説法，英式説法是 pedestrian crossing 或 zebra crossing。

 情境二：橫過馬路時

5. Mom, let's cross at the crosswalk.

   媽，我們走斑馬線／行人橫道吧。

6. Never cross the road if the walking man signal turns red.

   紅燈亮着時千萬不要橫過馬路。

7. Stop when the green light is flickering.

   綠燈閃爍的時候要停下來。

8. Look both ways before crossing any streets.

   過馬路時先要看看左右兩側。

 情境三：在行人路上

> **英文能力 UP！**
>
> Sidewalk 是美式説法，英式説法是 pavement。

9. Don't run on roads.

   在路上別跑。

10. Use the sidewalk to stay safe on the road.

    使用行人道，這樣才安全。

11. Never cross at a corner. Corners are the blind spots for drivers.

    不要在拐彎處過馬路，拐彎處是司機的盲點。

Scene 115

跟父母失散

Don't talk to strangers.
不要跟陌生人説話。

 Conversation 美國家庭這樣説

Mom: When you run away from Mommy in the store I feel worried because you could get lost.

Boy: Why?

迷路　　　　　　佔便宜

Mom: There are strangers who might take advantage of you.

Boy: Are they not friendly people?

Mom: Some are friendly, some are not. When I'm with you, you can be friendly and talk to strangers. But when I'm not with you, don't talk to strangers. Understood?

Boy: Okay.

家長手記 家長常問孩子是否明白，用英語來表達有以下方式：Do you understand?（你懂嗎？）/ Is that clear?（清楚了嗎？）/ You know what I mean?（你懂我的意思嗎？）/ Get the picture?（你了解情況嗎？）

Useful Expressions 活學活用

聆聽英文內容

 情境一：學會拒絕

1. If a stranger tries to give you something, say NO.
   如果有陌生人給你東西，要說不。

2. Don't take anything from strangers.
   別拿陌生人給你的東西。

3. Sorry, I can't take candy from you.
   不好意思，我不能要你的糖果。

4. I have to ask Mommy before I go with you.
   我要問准媽媽，才能跟你走。

5. What should I do if a stranger tries to grab me?
   如果有陌生人要把我抓走呢？

6. You need to get away quickly. Yell and make a loud scene. And RUN! If possible, run toward an adult and yell "Help! This is not my Dad!"
   你要馬上逃跑。大聲呼叫，然後跑！有可能的話，跑向一個大人身邊大叫：「救命！這個人不是我爸爸！」

 情境二：迷路了該怎麼辦？

7. If you get lost, don't panic. Stop where you are and yell.
   如果你迷路了，不要慌張，停下來大聲叫我。

8. Run to the nearest store and ask them to call the police.
   跑到最近的商店，請他們打電話報警。

 情境三：要怎樣求救？

9. I'm lost. Please help me find my mother.
   我迷路了，請你幫我找媽媽。

10. This is my parent's phone number, please call them.
    這是我爸爸媽媽的電話號碼，請打電話給他們。

Scene 116

受傷了

Your knee is bleeding.

你的膝蓋流血了。

💬 Conversation 美國家庭這樣說

Mom: What happened? Why are you crying?

Girl: I slipped on the floor.

Mom: Your palm got bruised. And your knee is bleeding.

Girl: That was a scary fall.

Mom: Calm down. That's a good girl. Don't cry. It's all right. Let me put the ointment on.

Girl: When can I get better?

Mom: Maybe in a week or so.

英文能力 UP！

What happened? 是口語裏常用來詢問別人怎麼了的慣用語。其他表示關心的慣用語還有：What's the matter with you?（你怎麼回事？）、What's wrong with you?（你哪裏不對勁？）、What happened to you?（你怎麼了？）

Useful Expressions 活學活用

 情境一：詢問受傷的原因

1. Did you get hit? Or did you just fall?

   你是給打傷的嗎？還是你跌倒了？

2. Where are you hurt?

   你哪裏受傷了？

3. Where did you get hurt?

   你是在哪裏弄傷的？

> **英文能力 UP！**
>
> 這兩句話的意思分別是 Which body part is hurting?（你身體哪一部分受傷了？）和 Where were you when you got hurt?（你受傷時在哪裏？）

 情境二：受傷了

4. I fell down.

   我摔倒了。

5. I tripped over my toys.

   我被玩具絆倒了。

6. I've got a cut here.

   我這裏被割傷了。

7. I sprained / twisted my ankle.

   我扭傷腳踝了。

8. I burned my hand.

   我的手燙傷了。

情境三：安撫受傷的孩子

9. Are you okay? Don't cry. It's all right.

   你沒事吧？別哭，沒事的。

10. How about a hug?

    抱一下好嗎？

11. I'll put a band-aid on.

    我幫你貼創可貼（膠布）。

家長手記

根據統計，騎腳踏車（cycling）是引起兒童交通意外受傷的主要原因之一。家長要多加留意呀！

Scene
117

颱風天
The hurricane is coming.
颱風要來了。

💬 Conversation 美國家庭這樣說

Girl: Why are you closing all the windows, Mommy?

Mom: The weather forecast says a hurricane is coming.

Girl: Is it going to rain soon?

Mom: Very likely. Come and help, we need to tape the windows. After that, I will need to go and buy more food.

Girl: Can I go with you?

Mom: No. You're safest at home.

英文能力 UP！

Hurricane（颶風）和我們說的 typhoon（颱風）名字不同，但其實是一樣的。
大西洋上生成的叫 hurricane，太平洋上生成的叫 typhoon，只是出現的地方
不同，才有了「颶風」與「颱風」兩個名字。

Useful Expressions 活學活用

聆聽英文內容

 情境一：颱風來了

1. Gosh, the wind is strong today.
   天啊！今天的風很大。

2. A powerful hurricane is coming.
   超強颱風要來了。

3. The wind is blowing so hard the trees are bending.
   風吹得很大，樹木都彎了。

4. Listen to the sounds. It's scary!
   聽聽這些聲音，很恐怖呀！

5. Mom, is it going to rain soon?
   媽，馬上要下雨嗎？

6. The weather forecast is for severe storms tonight.
   天氣報告說今晚會有暴風雨。

 情境二：做好安全措施

7. Let's close all the windows.
   我們來把所有窗戶都關上。

8. I'd better tape the windows.
   我最好用膠紙把窗戶貼好。

9. Let's move the plants inside.
   我們來把植物都移進室內。

英文能力 UP！

除了 storm 之外，與颱風有關的氣象單詞還有：thunderstorm（雷雨）、tornado / twister（龍捲風）。冬季雖然較少颱風，卻會出現 snowstorm / blizzard（暴風雪）。

 情境三：要外出的話

10. I'm going to buy some food.
    我去買些食物回來。

11. Be careful when you are out, Mom.
    媽，您外出時要小心呀。

Scene 118

乘搭升降機

Wait until everyone gets off.
先等所有人都出來。

💬 Conversation 美國家庭這樣說

Mom: Go and call the elevator.

Boy: OK. Mom, what floor are we going to?

Mom: 15th floor. Hey, don't lean on the elevator door. The door might open. You might also get stuck in the door.

夾住

Boy: Let's get in!

Mom: Wait until everyone gets off.

英文能力 UP！

形態動詞 might 表示推測，意思是「可能、也許」，例如：Someone might get in.（也許會有人進來。）

Useful Expressions 活學活用

 情境一：在升降機內

1. What floor should we press?

   我們要按哪一層呢？

2. Let me push the button.

   我來按按鈕。

3. Hold the elevator.

   讓升降機停一下。

4. Can you press the 10th floor?

   你能按一下 10 樓嗎？

5. Wow, it's moving fast.

   哇，好快啊。

6. Press the open / close button.

   按一下開門 / 關門按鈕。

7. Let's get out.

   我們出去吧。

情境二：遵守安全規則

8. I won't lean on the door.

   我不會倚着升降機門。

9. I won't jump inside the elevator.

   我不會在升降機內跳動。

10. Get off when the elevator is completely open.

    升降機門完全打開以後才出去。

11. In case of fire, do not use the lift.

    如遇火警，切勿使用升降機。

家長手記

城市的孩子容易發生升降機事故，他們受傷的原因主要來自升降機門開關時遭夾傷。家長要小心留意！

Scene 119

乘扶手電梯

Hold the handrail.
握着扶手。

💬 Conversation 美國家庭這樣説

Girl:　Mom, that girl is not tall enough to hold the handrail.

Mom:　Yes, she's too small. It may be several more years before she's ready to go it alone on the escalator.

Girl:　Ouch! That hurts!

Mom:　Oh, don't stand too close to the side of the escalator. That's dangerous! You could get your shoe, or shoelaces, caught between the steps and the sidewall. That would hurt you.

📎

英文能力 UP！

Ouch! 是擬聲詞，表示突然感到疼痛時「哎唷」的叫聲。其他表示痛楚的擬聲詞還有：Ow!（哎唷！）和 Ooh!（呵！）

Useful Expressions 活學活用

 情境一：提醒孩子注意安全

1. Face forward.
   面向前。

2. Grip the handrail.
   緊握扶手。

3. Pick up your feet!
   好好走路！

4. Lift your foot when stepping on and off the escalator to avoid losing your balance or getting your toes trapped.
   出入扶手電梯時應提步，以免失去重心跌倒，或夾住腳趾。

5. Why can't we stand too close to the side of the escalator?
   我們為什麼不能靠着扶手電梯邊？

6. Loose shoelaces or scarves can get trapped in the escalator.
   鬆了的鞋帶或頸巾可能會夾在扶手電梯裏的。

7. Do not stick the tip of your umbrella into the gap between the steps.
   不要把雨傘末端插在梯級之間的空隙內。

 情境二：做個好孩子

8. I can hold the handrail.
   我能夠握着扶手。

9. I won't run or play on the escalator.
   我不會在扶手電梯上亂跑或嬉戲。

10. I'm keeping my feet away from the sides.
    我的腳沒有碰到扶手電梯邊。

11. So my feet won't be caught in the gaps.
    因此我的腳不會被夾住。

251

Scene 120

有人敲門

Mom, Dad! Someone is at the door!

媽，爸！門口有人來了！

💬 Conversation 美國家庭這樣說

Boy: Mom, someone knocked on the door when you were away.

Mom: Who's that? Did you open the door?!

Boy: No, I didn't. I was scared, but I tried not to be.

Mom: Good boy. Remember, if you have no idea who it is, there's no way you should open the door to a stranger when you're home alone.

Boy: What should I do if he keeps ringing the doorbell?

Mom: Pretend you're yelling to Mom and Dad that someone is at the door. Like, "Mom, Dad! Someone is at the door!"

英文能力 UP！

No way 常用於口語，有「絕對不」的意思。如有人說：Come on, open the door!（來，開門吧！），就可以回答：No way!（不行！）

Useful Expressions 活學活用

聆聽英文內容

 情境一：外出前的囑咐

1. I'm going out, but I'll be back soon.
   我要外出一下，不過會很快回來。

2. Are you saying I need to be alone?
   你是說我必須單獨在家嗎？

3. Can't you be by yourself? You're a big boy / girl now.
   你不能自己單獨一人嗎？你已經長大了。

4. Call Mom if there's anything you need.
   有需要的話隨時給媽媽打電話。

5. Don't go anywhere with a grown-up unless Mommy or Daddy says it's okay.
   除非得到爸爸或媽媽的批准，否則不能跟陌生人外出。

6. I won't go outside until Mom comes back.
   媽媽回來之前，我都不會出去。

情境二：陌生人來敲門時

7. What if a stranger rings our doorbell?
   如果有陌生人按門鈴，那怎麼辦？

8. If you don't feel comfortable, don't answer the door.
   如果你覺得奇怪的話，不要開門。

9. Shall I pretend that I'm not home and keep particularly quiet?
   我要假裝不在家，不發出任何聲響嗎？

10. Just continue going about your normal activities inside. Reason being that if the stranger is a burglar, he may go ahead and break in if he thinks no one is home.
    乾脆繼續你在家裏的一切正常活動，因為如果那個陌生人是竊賊，當他以為我們家裏沒有人，可能會破門而入。

1 My Body
我的身體

可在學習
Scene 2 & 5
前或後，完成
這練習。

Are you growing bigger and taller? Measure your height and weight and fill in the blanks.

你的身高和體重是多少呢？請量度一下，並把它們記錄下來。

1. How tall are you?

   I am _____ cm tall.

2. How much do you weigh?

   I weigh _____ kg.

How many teeth do you have? Count and fill in the blanks. Draw an " ✗ " on the tooth you have lost, if any.

你有多少顆牙齒呢？請數一數你的牙齒數目，然後回答問題。如果你有牙齒脫落了，就在圖中加 ✗ 來表示。

3. How many teeth do you have?

   I have _____ teeth.

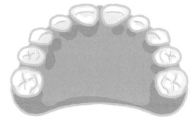

4. How many teeth have you lost?

   I have lost _____ tooth / teeth.

2 Daily Life
日常生活

可在學習
Theme 2
前或後，完成
這練習。

What does your daily routine look like? Talk about it. Use the pictures to help you.
你的日常生活是怎樣的呢？請參考以下的圖畫，説説看。

get up

eat breakfast

go to school

brush teeth

eat lunch

eat dinner

shower

go to bed

3 What's the Color?
這是什麼顏色？

可在學習
Scene 12
前或後，完成
這練習。

What colors are the clothes? Fill in the blanks.
這些衣服是什麼顏色的呢？請把答案填在橫線上。

1. My cap is _____ .

2. My T-shirt is _____ .

3. My skirt is _____ .

4. My shorts are _____ .

5. My trainers are _____ .

6. My shoes are _____ .

7. My scarf is _____ .

4 My Classmates
我的同學

可在學習
Scene 24
前或後，完成
這練習。

How well do you know your classmates? Write down their names if they meet the criteria.

你對你的同學認識有多少？請根據以下表格，找出符合條件的同學，把他們的名字寫下來吧。

Find a friend who ...

has a pet dog.	has a brother.
likes to play ball games.	can play an instrument.
has a sister.	likes the color blue.
likes ice cream.	is wearing glasses.

5 Healthy Diet
健康飲食

可在學習
Theme 4
前或後，完成
這練習。

You need to eat fruits, vegetables, grains, protein foods, and dairy to get the nutrients you need. What do you like to eat? Please tick (✔) your choices.

水果、蔬菜、穀類、蛋白質和奶類製品能組成健康的一餐。你今天想吃些什麼呢？請根據你的口味來為自己點餐，在適當的 ☐ 內加 ✔。

1. Fruits: ☐ apple ☐ orange ☐ grapes ☐ _____

2. Vegetables: ☐ potato ☐ carrot ☐ spinach ☐ _____

3. Grains: ☐ bread ☐ rice ☐ noodles ☐ _____

4. Protein: ☐ pork ☐ beef ☐ chicken ☐ _____

5. Dairy: ☐ milk ☐ cheese ☐ ice cream ☐ _____

6 Recycling
廢物回收

可在學習
Scene 37
前或後，完成
這練習。

Blue for waste paper, yellow for cans and brown for plastic. Can you put these into the recycling bins? Match.

藍色回收箱用來回收廢紙，黃色回收箱用來回收金屬廢物，而咖啡色回收箱用來回收塑料廢物。你能把這些廢物放進適當的回收箱嗎？請把代表正確答案的英文字母填在橫線上。

A.
B.
C.

D.
E.
F.

paper plastic cans

1. Blue bin:

_____

2. Brown bin:

_____

3. Yellow bin:

_____

259

親子小活動
Family Activity

7 Crossword
填字遊戲

可在學習
Scene 42
前或後，完成
這練習。

Let's do a crossword. Use the clues to help you.
我們一起來玩填字遊戲吧！請根據以下指示，完成填字遊戲。

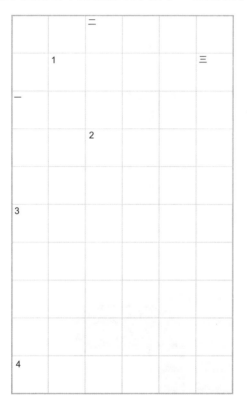

Across 1.   2.   3. 故事   4. hide and _____

Down   一.   二. 動畫片   三.

(is a game.)

8 Reading Fun
閱讀樂

可在學習
Scene 43
前或後，完成
這練習。

What kinds of books do you like to read? Please tick（✔）
and fill in the blanks.

以下是兒童書的一般分類，你喜歡看哪個類別呢？請在適當的 ☐ 內
加 ✔，然後回答問題。

☐ Sticker books   ☐ Adventures

☐ Picture books   ☐ Pop-up books

☐ Storybooks   ☐ Science fiction

☐ Fantasy   ☐ Comics

☐ Fairy tales   ☐ Folk tales and myths

My favorite book is _____ because _____

_____ .

261

9 Count and Draw
算算數，繪繪畫

可在學習
Scene 53 & 54
前或後，完成
這練習。

Do the sum for each problem. Then, color according to the key at the bottom.

請先計算圖中各題加數，然後根據答案的指示，填上適當的顏色，完成這幅特別的圖畫吧！

1. If the answers are 3 or 6, color the space red.

2. If the answers are 4 or 9, color the space green.

3. If the answers are 12 or 18, color the space blue.

10 Transportation
交通工具

可在學習
Scene 60 & 61
前或後，完成
這練習。

Can you name these vehicles? Draw lines to match them.
你知道這是什麼交通工具嗎？請配對一下，把正確的答案連起來。

car

bus

tram

ferry

truck

airplane

11 Directions 方向

可在學習
Scene 70
前或後，完成
這練習。

Which way is Water World? Read the conversation and draw the correct route.

「水世界」在哪裏呢？請根據以下對話，在地圖中找出「水世界」的位置，把路線畫出來。

A: Excuse me, how do I get to Water World?

B: Go to the corner. Turn left. It's on the right, opposite the museum.

12 Postcard
明信片

可在學習
Scene 72
前或後，完成
這練習。

When you are away on holiday, it can be nice to write some postcards to your friends and family. Who would you write to? Now, write a postcard to them.

假如你現在在外地旅遊，你想寄一張明信片回國，你會寄給誰？
請把你要説的話寫下來吧。

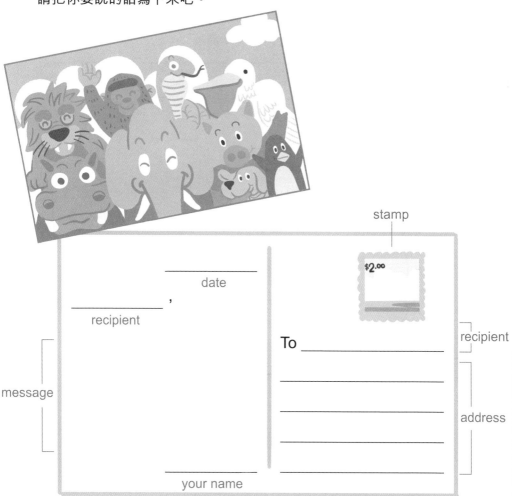

stamp

$2.00

_____
date

_____,
recipient

message

To _____

_____ recipient

_____ address

_____
your name

13 Christmas Card 聖誕卡

可在學習
Scene 79
前或後，完成
這練習。

All over the world, children write letters and cards to Santa Claus, letting him know what they would like for Christmas. Now, write and draw your own Christmas card to Santa.

我們來給聖誕老人寫張聖誕卡，把你的聖誕願望告訴他吧！請你在聖誕卡上半部畫出你希望收到的聖誕禮物，然後在卡的下半部寫下你的聖誕願望。寫好以後，記住寫上你的名字啊！

This is the Christmas present I wish to receive …

Dear Santa,

All I want for Christmas is

_____

Love,

_____

14 Introduce Yourself
自我介紹

可在學習 Scene 83 前或後，完成 這練習。

Can you introduce yourself? Create a poster that's all about you. Add your name, age, favorite things, etc. Then, present it to people so they get to know you.

你可以用英語介紹一下自己嗎？只要在以下表格填上你的資料，然後把這些內容讀出來，那就是一遍完整的自我介紹了。

All about me

My name is _____ . I am _____ years old.

People in my family:

My favorite food:

My favorite color:

My favorite sport:

My likes:

1. _____

2. _____

3. _____

My dislikes:

1. _____

2. _____

3. _____

If I could have any animal in the world for a pet, it would be a / an:

15 My Dream
我的夢想

可在學習
Scene 96
前或後，完成
這練習。

What do you want to be when you grow up? Think about it. What will be your answer?

你有沒有想過你長大以後會做什麼呢？你喜歡以下職業嗎？請想一想，然後把你的志願寫下來。

police officer   firefighter   doctor   teacher

scientist   astronaut   chef   singer

When I grow up, I want to be a / an _____ . It is

because _____ .

16 Be Polite!
有禮貌的孩子！

可在學習
Scene 103
前或後，完成
這練習。

Are you a well-mannered child? Do you like to receive these "polite and well-mannered stickers"? Here's a list of things to get started. Please tick (✔) if you are ready to do these things.

對於有禮貌、守規矩的孩子，美國的老師會給他們送「有禮貌貼紙」作為獎勵。如果你能做到以下的事情，請在 ☐ 內加 ✔。

1. ☐ I am polite.

2. ☐ I say "Please".

3. ☐ I am kind to others.

4. ☐ I say "Sorry".

5. ☐ I say "Thank you".

6. ☐ I share with others.

7. ☐ I take turns.

8. ☐ I help others.

17 I Need a Doctor!
我要看醫生！

可在學習
Scene 109
前或後，完成
這練習。

What's wrong with you? Fill in the blanks.
你哪裏不舒服嗎？請把答案填在橫線上。

nose   legs   eyes   chest   throat
tongue   headache   stomachache

1. My _____ are dry.

2. My _____ is runny.

3. My _____ is sore.

4. My _____ feels tight.

5. I have a _____ .

6. I cut my _____ .

7. I have a _____ .

8. My _____ feel weak.

18 Getting Hurt
受傷了

可在學習
Scene 116
前或後，完成
這練習。

What happened to you? Match the pictures with the correct sentences.

你怎麼了？請把圖片和文字連接起來吧。

1. • • A. I got stung by a bee.

2.  • • B. I've got a cut.

3. • • C. I sprained my ankle.

4.  • • D. I got burned.

5.  • • E. I have a cramp.

親子小活動 Family Activity 答案

Activity 3
1. My cap is <u>red</u>.
2. My T-shirt is <u>green</u>.
3. My skirt is <u>orange</u>.
4. My shorts are <u>blue</u>.
5. My trainers are <u>yellow</u>.
6. My shoes are <u>brown</u>.
7. My scarf is <u>pink</u>.

Activity 6
1. Blue bin：C、D
2. Brown bin：A、E
3. Yellow bin：B、F

Activity 7
Across
1. paper
2. TV
3. story
4. seek

Down
一 . scissors
二 . cartoon
三 . rock

Activity 9

Activity 10

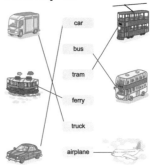

Activity 11

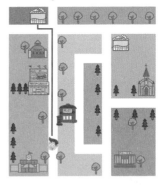

Activity 17
1. My <u>eyes</u> are dry.
2. My <u>nose</u> is runny.
3. My <u>throat</u> is sore.
4. My <u>chest</u> feels tight.
5. I have a <u>headache</u>.
6. I cut my <u>tongue</u>.
7. I have a <u>stomachache</u>.
8. My <u>legs</u> feel weak.

Activity 18
1. C   2. B
3. A   4. E
5. D

Theme 1

Growing Up
身體的部位怎麼說？

Learn these words and phrases

不同的人種，除了膚色、髮色，或面部骨骼結構有所不同之外，他們的身體部位都是一樣的啊。

你知道自己身體的各個部位怎麼說嗎？

正面

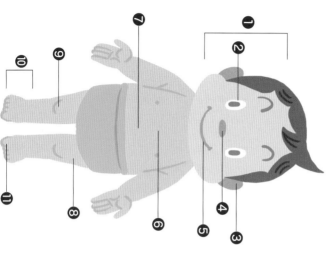

1 face 臉部
2 eye 眼睛
3 ear 耳朵
4 nose 鼻子
5 mouth 嘴巴
6 chest 胸部
7 stomach 腹部
8 leg 腿
9 knee 膝蓋
10 foot 腳
11 toe 腳趾

背面

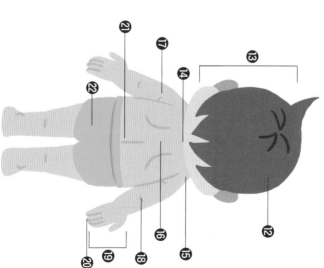

12 hair 頭髮
13 head 頭
14 neck 頸
15 shoulder 肩膀
16 back 背部
17 arm 手臂
18 elbow 手肘
19 hand 手
20 finger 手指
21 waist 腰
22 bottom 屁股

Theme 2

Daily Routines
美國孩子平常的早上怎麼過？

Learn these words and phrases

很多美國家庭都會為孩子制定「我一天的計劃」（My Daily Routines），把早上和晚上要做的事情清楚列出來。

你早上的計劃又是怎樣的呢？

早上

❶ potty 上廁所
❷ wash face 洗臉
❸ brush teeth 刷牙
❹ comb hair 梳理頭髮
❺ make bed 整理牀舖
❻ get dressed 換衣服
❼ eat breakfast 吃早餐
❽ shoes and school bag 穿鞋子，拿書包
❾ say goodbye 說再見
❿ off to school 出門上學去

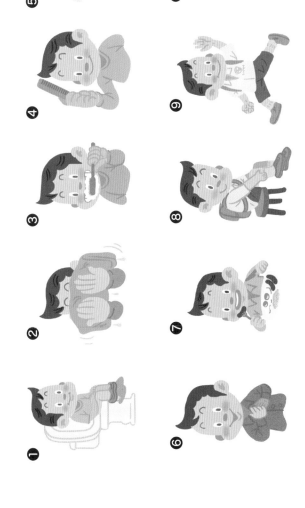

Daily Routines
美國孩子平常的晚上怎麼過？

ABC 詞彙手帳 Vocabulary

Learn these words and phrases

很多美國家庭都會為孩子制定「我一天的計劃」(My Daily Routines)，把早上和晚上要做的事情清楚列出來。你晚上的計劃又是怎樣的呢？

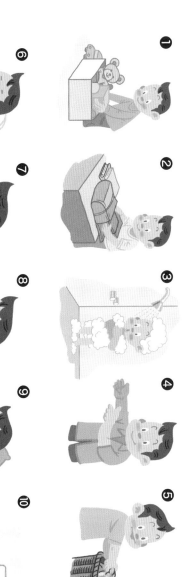

晚上

1. pick up toys 整理玩具
2. pack school bag 收拾書包
3. shower 洗澡
4. put on pajama 換睡衣
5. put dirty clothes in hamper 把髒衣服放進洗衣籃
6. potty 上廁所
7. wash face 洗臉
8. brush teeth 刷牙
9. go to bed 上牀睡覺
10. lights out 關燈

詞彙手帳 Vocabulary

Learn these words and phrases

看看你的書包，除了書本和文具外，
還放了些什麼？

1 book 書本
2 exercise book 練習簿
3 pencil case 筆盒
4 pencil 鉛筆
5 mechanical pencil 鉛芯筆
　（英式 propelling pencil）
6 colored pencil 顏色筆
7 highlighter 螢光筆
8 crayon 蠟筆
9 pencil sharpener 捲筆刀 (鉛筆刨)
10 eraser 橡皮 (英式 rubber)
11 ruler 尺
12 paper 紙張
13 paper clip 曲別針 (萬字夾)
14 glue 膠水
15 stapler 釘書機
16 scissors 剪刀
17 water bottle 水壺

Food and Dining
西式早餐吃什麼?

ABC 詞彙手帳 Vocabulary

Learn these words and phrases

吃一頓豐富的早餐,有助孩子上學集中精神。美國孩子一般會在家裏吃早餐,一起看看他們會吃什麼吧!

❶ a cup of tea 一杯茶
❷ a glass of milk 一杯牛奶
❸ a glass of orange juice 一杯橙汁
❹ toast with jam 果醬吐司 (果醬多士)
❺ toast with cheese 奶酪吐司 (芝士多士)
❻ butter 牛油
❼ marmalade 橘子醬
❽ oatmeal 燕麥片粥 (英式 porridge)
❾ cereal 穀類食物
❿ bacon and eggs 煙肉和蛋
⓫ scrambled eggs 炒蛋
⓬ bread 麵包
⓭ sandwiches 三明治 (三文治)
⓮ biscuits 餅乾
⓯ pancakes 煎餅 (班戟)
⓰ syrup 糖漿
⓱ fruit salad 水果沙拉 (水果沙律)

Theme 5

Household Chores
美國孩子會做哪些家務？

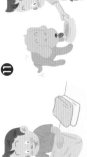

詞彙手帳 ABC Vocabulary

Learn these words and phrases

美國家庭有一個孩子的「適齡家務清單」（Age Appropriate Chores Chart），清單中列出不同年齡的孩子可以幫忙做哪些家務。你也試試來幫忙吧！

較年幼的孩子

❶ stack books 擺好書本
❷ match socks 配對襪子
❸ put away laundry 把洗好的衣物放好
❹ empty wastebaskets 清理廢紙箱的垃圾
❺ get the newspaper 拿報紙
❻ water plants 給植物澆水

孩子長大了一點

❼ set / clear table 擺好 / 收拾餐桌
❽ clean bathroom sink 清潔廁所洗臉盆
❾ sort laundry 把衣服分類
❿ fold clothes 摺衣服
⓫ feed pets 餵飼寵物

Theme 6

Relaxing at Home
美國電視節目有哪些類別？

ABC 詞彙手帳 Vocabulary

美國電視節目的分類繁多，各適其適，你最喜歡看的電視節目是什麼呢？

Learn these words and phrases

❶ cartoon 卡通
❷ sports 體育運動
❸ game show 遊戲節目
❹ documentary 紀錄片
❺ news 新聞
❻ music 音樂
❼ movie 電影
❽ travel or holiday 旅遊或度假節目
❾ fashion 時裝
❿ food 飲食
⓫ animal or wildlife 動物或野生世界
⓬ charity 慈善籌款節目
⓭ soap 肥皂劇
⓮ talk show 清談節目

Theme 7

Extracurricular Activities
哪些興趣班最受美國孩子歡迎？

體育是美國民族文化一個重要的組成部分，許多孩子在選擇課外活動或興趣班時，都會以體育運動為主。以下這些課外活動或興趣班，你最喜歡哪一項呢？

Learn these words and phrases

badminton
羽毛球

swimming
游泳

ballet
芭蕾舞

gymnastics
體操

ice skating
滑冰

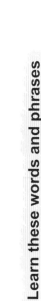

drawing
繪畫

violin
小提琴

soccer
足球
(英式 football)

rugby
橄欖球

softball
壘球

baseball
棒球

golf
高爾夫球

tennis
網球

table tennis
乒乓球

Theme 8

Hanging Out
美國超級市場的貨架有哪些分類？

Learn these words and phrases

超級市場裏的貨品包羅萬象，林林總總。為了方便顧客選購貨品，所有貨品都會各歸其類，擺放在不同的貨架上。

fruits
水果

vegetables
蔬菜

meat
肉類

seafood
海鮮

beverages
飲料

egg and dairy products
蛋及奶類製品

snacks and candy
零食及糖果

canned food
罐頭食品

frozen food
冷藏食品

bread and bakery
麵包糕點

breakfast items
早餐食品

household products
家居用品

詞彙手帳
Vocabulary

Theme 9

Traveling
你去過這些國家或城市旅遊嗎？

Learn these words and phrases

世界上共有 224 個國家或城市，以下這些國家和城市，你有去過嗎？

China
中國

Hong Kong
香港

South Korea
南韓

Japan
日本

Singapore
新加坡

Malaysia
馬來西亞

Thailand
泰國

Australia
澳洲

United Kingdom
英國

Germany
德國

Spain
西班牙

Netherlands
荷蘭

Egypt
埃及

Brazil
巴西

Canada
加拿大

United States
of America
美國

Special Days
你認識與聖誕節有關的詞語嗎？

ABC 詞彙手帳 Vocabulary

Learn these words and phrases

聖誕節是紀念耶穌（Jesus Christ）降生的節日，也是西方最重要的節日之一。以下這些與聖誕節有關的常用詞彙，你認識多少個呢？

❶ snowman 雪人
❷ reindeer 馴鹿
❸ Christmas tree 聖誕樹
❹ angel 天使
❺ candy cane 拐杖糖
❻ Christmas present 聖誕禮物
❼ stocking 長筒襪
❽ snowflake 雪花
❾ bell 鈴鐺
❿ Santa Claus 聖誕老人
⓫ Christmas card 聖誕卡
⓬ pudding 布丁
⓭ gingerbread 薑餅
⓮ candle 蠟燭

ABC 詞彙手帳 Vocabulary

Theme 11

Be Courteous
收到別人送的玩具時要說什麼？

Learn these words and phrases

以下這些玩具當中，你最喜歡的是哪一種呢？如果你收到別人送給你的玩具，一定要禮貌地向對方說一聲 Thank you（謝謝）啊！

blocks
積木

yo-yo
溜溜球（搖搖）

hula hoop
呼啦圈

whistle
哨子

doll
洋娃娃

toy car
玩具車

jigsaw puzzle
拼圖

jump rope
跳繩

water gun
水槍

ball
球

robot
機械人

teddy bear
玩具熊

tricycle
三輪車

Thank you for your present!

Theme 12

Communication
你會用什麼詞彙表達今天的心情？

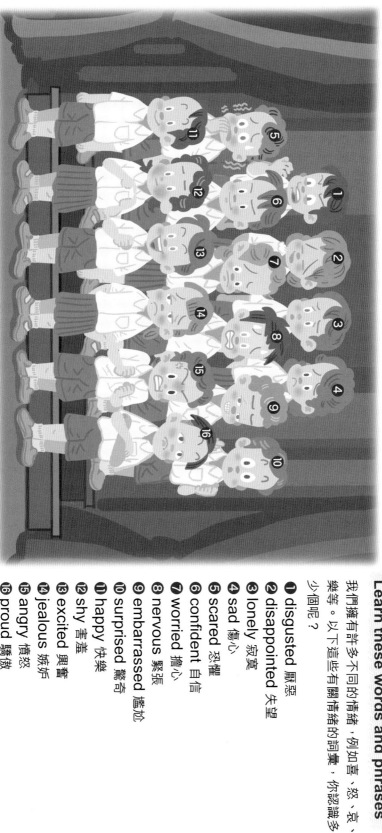

ABC 詞彙手帳 Vocabulary

Learn these words and phrases

我們擁有許多不同的情緒，例如喜、怒、哀、樂等。以下這些有關情緒的詞彙，你認識多少個呢？

❶ disgusted 厭惡
❷ disappointed 失望
❸ lonely 寂寞
❹ sad 傷心
❺ scared 恐懼
❻ confident 自信
❼ worried 擔心
❽ nervous 緊張
❾ embarrassed 尷尬
❿ surprised 驚奇
⓫ happy 快樂
⓬ shy 害羞
⓭ excited 興奮
⓮ jealous 妒忌
⓯ angry 憤怒
⓰ proud 驕傲

Theme 13

Did something Good or Bad
美國家長喜歡或討厭孩子哪些行為？

習慣（habits）是慢慢養成的，不良的習慣一旦養成，要想改變過來就不容易了。要做一個討人喜歡的孩子，就必須馬上把所有壞習慣和行為都戒掉啊！

Learn these words and phrases

喜歡的
行為

brushing twice
早晚刷牙

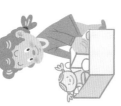
sleeping on time
準時睡覺

saying please
and thank you
說請和謝謝

picking up after
themselves
自己收拾

smiling
微笑

sharing
分享

討厭的
行為

sucking thumb
吮拇指

picking nose
挖鼻孔

biting nails
咬手指

spitting
隨地吐痰

yelling
大喊大叫

lying
說謊

Theme 14

Being Sick
你哪裏不舒服嗎？

Learn these words and phrases

我們生病的時候，身體會出現不同的症狀，醫生會根據這些症狀來為我們診斷治療，對症下藥。以下這些症狀都是比較常見的，你能說出來嗎？

headache
頭痛

fever
發燒

runny nose
流鼻水

sneeze
打噴嚏

stuffy nose
鼻塞

sore throat
喉嚨痛

cough
咳嗽

headache
頭痛

cold
感冒

backache
背痛

stomachache
肚子痛

dizzy
頭暈

vomit
嘔吐

toothache
牙痛

drowsy
昏昏欲睡

Cautions
你有遵守安全規則嗎？

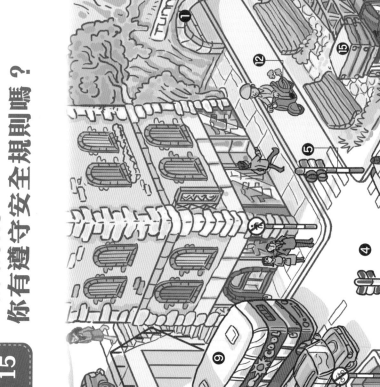

ABC 詞彙手帳 Vocabulary

Learn these words and phrases

在繁忙的街道上，不論行人、車輛都要相互尊重，大家才能有安全的交通環境。就行人來說，走路時要走行人道、過馬路時要遵守交通規則，這樣才能確保安全啊！

1. tunnel 隧道
2. subway 行人隧道
3. bridge 橋
4. road 道路
5. traffic lights 交通燈
6. crosswalk 行人橫道
7. sidewalk 行人道（英式 pavement）
8. car 汽車
9. bus 巴士
10. bicycle 自行車
11. pedestrian 行人
12. motorcycle 摩托車
13. road sign 交通標誌
14. police car 警車
15. fire engine 消防車